Cold War II

CATHY TRAVIS

Cold War II

CATHY TRAVIS

ISBN: 978-0-9974963-6-9

DEDICATION

For all of those who love constitutional democracy –
and free and fair elections.
For JJ, who asked me the next morning, "What happened?"
And for Vickie, who asked me at Christmas, "How bad can
this get?" (I still don't know)

LEGAL DISCLAIMER

This book is fiction. While some parts of the story line are true, nearly all characters are fictional. Only two characters are based on an actual person.

If anyone worries a character is based on them, the author is happy to rewrite a description of that character to employ a legal literary premise; see more here:

https://en.wikipedia.org/wiki/Small_penis_rule.

This book is provided and sold with the knowledge that the publisher and author do not offer any legal or other professional evidence in any matter under investigation.

This book does not contain all information available on the subject. This book has not been created to be specific to any individual's or organizations' situation or needs. Every effort has been made to make the text as accurate as possible. However, there may be typographical errors.

The author and publisher shall have no liability or responsibility to any person or entity regarding any loss or damage incurred, or alleged to have incurred, directly or indirectly, by the information contained in this book. You hereby agree to be bound by this disclaimer or you may return this book within the guaranteed time period for a full refund.

Constitution Translated for Kids

By Cathy Travis

Constitution Translated for Kids - winner of the 2011 Gelett Burgess Children's Book Award for Education (Government and Politics), the "Mom's Choice Award" and a "Best Books Award" - is a simple, widely acclaimed, non-ideological translation of the entire U.S. Constitution, side-by-side with the original 1787 text. Teachers hail the accompanying free Teacher's Guide as an extraordinary resource to teach the Constitution to all ages.

Available in Spanish.

For free classroom resources, go to:

http://www.travisbooks.com/constitution-for-kids/

CONTENTS

FORWARD

I'm a political pro. Having spent 25 years on Capitol Hill
and in dozens of campaigns, I know the math of states
and districts.
I know profoundly that sometimes the other guys win.
That's democracy.
Ever since the stupor after the November 2016 election, I
wanted to explain how it happened through fiction.
Although you may recognize certain events, this is a
fictional tale told around true events – one that I hope my
fellow citizens can take as a cautionary tale.
At first, I thought I'd wait on more real investigation,
since the FBI investigation into Russian interference in
the 2016 election began in July 2016.
Then it occurred to me: we are never going to know
what all happened.
So I started with what I knew and fictionalized the
investigation we now know was going on as voters were
choosing sides throughout 2016.
Investigators and investigations are always the thing we
know the least about. They are always secret – and in
2016 – there were international spies helping the FBI try
to find proof our election was being fixed.
The only component of COLD WAR II that is not part
of the public record, or emerging as part of the public
record (as this book goes to print) is the Russian "boots"
component.
Here's why: every national security professional I know
who can't say stuff is busting to say … something.

Something that is so far unknown. But what do we not
know about? Possible tapes with compromising financial
information and … other things? Benefitting from
Russian money bigly over the years?
Some level of collusion between an adversarial Russia and
people around the President?
But we've heard about all of that. So there's something
else. Something so far-fetched, it's just not believable.
Something we can't hear because there's no way to fix it.
So I added a far-fetched, unbelievable story line.
The Russians who are the guiltiest of stealing our 2016
election are – by the way – far outside the reach of our
traditional law enforcement.
The damage to our body politic – our democracy, the
constitution, the rule of law, reason in public discourse,
and our centrist global political leadership – will all take a
long time to heal.
But healing begins with understanding what happened to
all of us.
Americans have remade ourselves after tragedy or farce
before. This moment is both.
Let's get busy.

CT

ORIGINS

December 10, 2011; Moscow, Russia, Red Square

American spy Jules Archer called Washington, D.C. from the street in the midst of an anti-government protest – the rarity of which made it a historical event.

Tens of thousands of Russians were protesting on their own streets, carrying signs and chanting unkind things about their president.

"You should have drone footage," she said quickly. "Estimating close to 50,000 protesters on the streets."

She glanced across the road at a policeman and a protester. The two parted company happily.

"No arrests so far that I've heard about," Jules said. "If that holds, it'll be new. We've got similar protests in over 70 cities across the country."

The voice from phone asked, "Does that threaten President Tutin's control of the Kremlin?"

"Waaaay too soon to say. This is still developing," she said carefully.

The Kremlin, President's Private Office

"THAT BITCH!" The Russian president fumed, watching the coverage of the uprisings. The dozen people in the room watched the red-faced president uneasily.

A tightly-controlled former spy, he rarely indulged in frustrated anger. Especially publicly.

U.S. Secretary of State Hailey Clanton was the target of his fury.

"Fucking Hailey Clanton did this," he snarled. He paced to the window to see the people with their signs on the street in front of the building.

"She is running massive influence operation against Mother Russia. It will not stand," he said ominously.

"How, sir?" asked an aide softly.

"She just gave all that money to rebel groups posing as 'pro-democracy' organizations. That was her signal," the president said, in a tone that suggested his conclusion not be questioned.

Silence in the room was broken by the protestors' chants, all of them mortifying to the Russian president.

The terrified advisors in the room eyed each other nervously. Nobody else said a word.

"This is the last time," the president said aloud, but to nobody in particular.

December 11, 2011; U.S. Embassy, Secure Room

Jules Archer sat in front of a screen, updating her boss back in Washington.

"A lawyer here organized the uprising on social media," she said. "But Tutin's bloggers bombarded his hashtags, kept 'em from merging at the Kremlin."

"Lawyer dead yet?" asked the voice from the screen.

"Not yet. At best, he'll be arrested."

"Anything else?"

"Tutin's really pissed at the Secretary. A source in the room with him said he pointedly blamed her."

* * * *

Later that night, Moscow flat of Jules Archer

Jules walked to the window of her Moscow flat, watching the street, as was her habit.

From Atlanta, Georgia, the daughter of a widowed father (her mother died when she was a baby), Jules' four older brothers toughened her up from an early age, teaching her to shoot and compete in sports.

A thin little thing, she was a surprisingly rough competitor, and a state champion in distance running.

The family business was law enforcement.

Her father was a county sheriff outside Atlanta. One brother founded a private security company; one served as a Lieutenant in the state police; and another walked the streets of Atlanta as a beat officer for the APD.

The family black sheep was the youngest brother, and the one Jules was closest to, Max, a star math student who worked on Wall Street right out of college.

A natural linguist, she gravitated towards the FBI, but not so much the bust-down-the doors stereotype. She wanted to work on international financial crimes and focus on the Russian mob.

The smart, petite teenager doubled down on school, completing her senior year in high school at the same time as her first year of Emory University, online. She truncated college, finishing up in two and a half years, and went directly to Emory's law school.

She'd barely begun her FBI career when the CIA came recruiting for her. She was publicly fired and hung out to dry by the FBI – all by design for her CIA cover.

Going forward, she was an FBI-trained security consultant, defrocked and humiliated by her old Bureau.

Six months later, she was at her new station out of the U.S. Embassy in Moscow.

Jules was really good at it.

She made friends all over: students, mobbed up Russians, oligarchs, people who worked for oligarchs, bankers, clerks, waiters, drivers and hundreds of other inside sources for Russia's government, banks and mob.

She knew the men who ran these institutions, and their intentions toward the U.S. and the western alliance.

Being a woman in a man's world helped more than she thought it would.

Jules could just as easily ooze teenage girl innocence as she could ooze hot sexuality.

Women liked and envied her, men wanted to fuck her. They all underestimated her.

If it weren't possible to fuck her, the men Jules spied on certainly enjoyed her natural beauty, flirting with her, and just being in her orbit.

They knew her as a disgraced FBI agent who just wanted to make money now.

She told those who asked why she was fired that she'd slept with the commander at Quantico, who'd passed her through the academy when she didn't make the grade.

It was a great cover; exactly why the FBI would fire someone, plus it highlighted sex and corruption, all of which Russians loved to believe about the U.S.

When she spoke Russian at all, she deliberately struggled with words, phrases, conjugating verbs … slowly and painfully mispronouncing words. All to make any bad guys comfortable speaking in Russian around her without realizing she'd hear everything her body mic could pick up.

She found herself privy to whispered phone conversations, drunken bragging or slips, and documents that informed U.S. government national security policy.

Soon, she was in the coolest job nobody could ever

know about: a highly successful spy.

Her older brothers knew only that she'd left the FBI and worked private security in Europe and Russia.

Only her father and Max in her family knew she was still an active U.S. agent, and that her firing was the cover story that would keep her alive in some pretty dangerous international neighborhoods.

She was just too much of a child of the law to let them all believe she'd disgraced the family business.

December 12, 2011; New York City, New York

Alex Splater sipped his coffee from his luxury high-rise in Woody Worldwide on Fifth Avenue. The Russian-born investor answered his phone. "Uncle, I was just reading about the unpleasantness there. So sad."

"This is why I call you," said his uncle, Antony Sopranov, a mobbed up Russian banker. The Russian oligarch closest to Russian President Vadik Tutin, Sopranov was a trim 63-year-old, and a to-the-point kind of guy.

"Our American friend from Tumultus — set up meeting with him, please," Sopranov said, the entire reason for the highly unusual call. "Where we were before. You know time and day, right?"

"Yes, Uncle Antony. It will be good to sit together again," Splater said. Smiling, the men hung up.

Moscow, Russia; Sopranov's Luxury Penthouse

Antony Sopranov frowned as he sloshed his bourbon, leaning against his fireplace. It was snowing outside.

The outburst by his old friend the president about the American Secretary of State was not necessarily a surprise.

But it was a little too public for his taste.

The protests had shaken all of them just a little bit.

Sopranov, the son of an oligarch from St. Petersburg, was a childhood friend of Tutin. Both were fans of Sambo (Soviet martial arts) and judo … making money … and ruling the world.

They went to different universities, and in different directions.

Sopranov, bored by school, spent more time than he should have improving his Sambo moves, and felt stifled by his father's lucrative business empire.

He was drawn to the black market in the late 1980s/early 1990s and the Russian mob, which would soon consume most of the Russian economy.

As he moved further into the world of Russian's international mafia, he learned that stealing and smuggling brought more wealth than he could possibly hide.

He hooked up again with his childhood friend, Tutin, in Germany when he was on an "economic mission" in Dresden, East Germany, in 1986. Sopranov began dropping in on Tutin regularly during his forays into Europe looking for "business" opportunities.

In the 1990s, he realized a banker could steal even more, easily launder and invest his money – PLUS – take a cut of the world's mob money just by laundering it.

He perfected the art of laundering the mob's money – legally – in cash exchanges from the United States Federal Reserve.

But all that was nowhere near his greatest achievement to date: Operation Tumultus, a secret plan to influence politics, business dealings, and news coverage inside the United States, Europe, and former Soviet republics – all to benefit Tutin's government.

The sun shone brightly, that day, six years before the protests soiled the streets of his beloved Moscow.

Summertime, 2005; Moscow, Russia, The Kremlin

Sopranov walked into the room with Kent Mantribe, a former legend of Republican U.S. presidential campaigns, now a U.S. lobbyist and political consultant.

"Never knew it was so hot here," said Mantribe, laying down a paper on the table dated July 8, 2005, headlined: "*Train Bombs Ignite London, al Qaeda Takes Credit.*"

Sopranov began introducing him to the oligarchs.

* * * *

Sitting at a large table, Mantribe began his briefing.

"Russia has not reached out via public relations, to make friends and influence people where you need it most," he smiled, watching Sopranov hand documents to the others.

"This is a multifaceted plan to influence politics, business, and news coverage inside the U.S., Europe, and the former Soviet republics – all to benefit Russia."

Smiles and nods around the room, as the men looked through the document.

* * * *

That 2005 meeting began a long and beneficial relationship for Sopranov and Mantribe around manipulating western nations, shaping them to a friendlier view of Russia and her intentions.

Sopranov began to realize his ambitious childhood dream – to rule the world, albeit from behind the scenes.

Mantribe pocketed more money than he ever thought was humanly possible.

December 13, 2011; Moscow flat of Jules Archer

In her robe and house shoes, as the sun began to rise over Moscow, Jules carried coffee to her laptop to check for any overnight activity on a multitude of taps she kept on Russian targets.

The screen flashed up a dozen-ish calls to listen to.

She scrolled down to the Sopranov call and put an earbud in. The mobster-banker and childhood friend of the president was hard to find making his own calls, and he usually talked in code.

She listened to the call with narrowed eyes, looking a little astonished, then concerned. She pursed her lips, opened her email and sent a message to an old friend from the FBI, Zack Tolliver.

10 p.m., New York City, NY, Brownstone of Zack Tolliver

Zack ate Chinese out of a box with chopsticks as he scrolled down his emails on his laptop at the window overlooking the street below, MSNBC blaring on TV.

The note from Jules popped up and he got a burst of adrenalin when he saw the subject line: "I miss you."

Smiling, he opened it and decrypted it.

"Wanna hook up?"

Smiling and nodding, he leaned back, hands behind his head remembering a moment during their training.

January, 2005; Quantico Naval Base, FBI Obstacle Course

Zack and Jules were running along the obstacle course,

far ahead of their classmates. Both excellent runners, they were improving their times on this course every day.

Zack pulled Jules off the trail to kiss her. Kissing him back, she pushed him up against a tree, pinning him there.

"Never stop till the race is over," she hissed breathlessly, and then dashed off. Zack stayed close, but she edged him out at the finish line.

10 p.m., New York City; Queens Brownstone of Zack Tolliver

Zack ran his hand over his mouth and around to massage his neck.

He sent a message back. "Miss u 2. Meet you there."

He looked down at the mime across the street mystifying tourists. Zack narrowed his eyes.

Then he shifted. Just a note from Jules and he was already horny.

October, 2007; New York City, NY, Manhattan Restaurant

Dinner was mostly finished, Zack and Jules were both holding wine.

"Here's to finally being done with Operation Wooden Nickel," Zack said.

"First night in a while we're not digging through dusty evidence rooms. I think this is the first non-takeout dinner since I got here."

"Then here's to getting out."

Their heads close, she rubbed the back of her hand against the back of his hand.

She bored in on his eyes, teasing, all hot.

"If we're celebrating, shall we take out dessert?"

Zack signaled the waiter.

New York City, New York; Jules' hotel room

Moving and heaving under the covers Zack and Jules orgasmed loudly.

Jules threw back the covers, astride him.

"Now I'm hot." She slid off him.

"I'll say," smiled Zack lazily.

"I meant —"

"I know. I'll get us some water."

He strode across the room, grabbed two waters, tossed one to her and got back under the covers.

They snuggled together.

"You know, if you ever wanna transfer to New York, there's always room for you on the financial crimes task force."

Jules took a long drink and looked sideways at him, deciding if she should tell him.

"What?" Zack asked.

"Need to tell you … hang on."

She picked up her phone, pushed the 'soundless' app, activating a wireless white zone that killed any electronic listening devices within a ten foot area.

"We gotta be soundless?"

"I got recruited by the CIA – linguistic skills, financial crimes training, and FBI experience," she said quickly. "Now that this is wrapped, I'm going to be publicly fired as an FBI agent to set up my cover in Moscow."

"Jules. Wow. Oh, that's why you never signed reports. Thanks, defense coulda come back at us on appeal."

"Hey, I'm a law brat, remember?"

Still hot, she threw off the covers and laid on her stomach, up on her elbows.

"They gotta take you down publicly, babe?" he asked, rubbing her butt.

"Yeah," she laughed at his naivety. "I'm an easy-to-find FBI agent. My dad and Max know. Now you know. That's actually bigger than I want that circle to be."

"When you leave?"

"Friday. Four months in Langley, then Moscow. Listen, I'll be doing financial crimes, Russian mob stuff. If I ever send you a message saying I miss you – I may well miss you, but if I say that, it's a signal to meet in person. There's a Hilton at the Frankfurt airport. I'll meet you there in 24 hours from your response."

"Understood. So, Friday, huh? That gives us a couple of days to keep doing this."

He dove under the covers, head between her legs.

Jules giggled and sucked in her breath.

TUMULTUS

December 14, 2011; Frankfurt, Germany, Airport Hilton

Zack smiled at Jules across the bar. He just couldn't help remembering their last encounter. This was the first time she'd used that code with him, so this must be big.

She waved at him, walked toward him, drink in hand.

She pecked him on the cheek. "This way," she pointed.

They walked in her room and he threw his coat and backpack on the couch.

She punched an electronic device to white out the conversation.

He sat down on the bed, patting it.

"This brings back memories. You know, it was a long plane ride. I'm a little horny."

"Well, that may not last."

He looked surprised, and stood up. He lifted his chin as in, 'what is it?'

"I caught a call made by Antony Sopranov in Moscow to his nephew Alex Splater in New York two days ago."

Zack whistled in appreciation. "Didn't think he ever made his own calls."

"Here's my report."

He read the very short summary. Slowly, and again.

"So, place, time and date are all prearranged."

"Not unlike this," she smiled.

His face acknowledged the irony. "Ideas on who the American is?"

"No idea."

"Where's Tumultus?"

"Don't think it's a place. So far, I've found it as the name of a book. It was a state of emergency decreed by ancient Rome. Word itself is Latin for invasion. It's similar to a name in Russian literature."

"Which you read in the original Russian, right?"

"You lose so much in translation," she snarked. "My guess is Tumultus was a Russian op, but haven't figured it out yet. When's the next flight back to New York?"

"There's one out in six hours."

"You crossed paths with Splater before?"

"Enough to know he's mobbed up the ass and been directing Russian money into New York real estate for over a decade through Prevezon Holdings. Haven't caught him doing anything illegal yet. He's careful."

"He's deep into Dale Woody, which is probably why he passed on the 2012 race."

Dale Woody, a brash casino developer and minor celebrity, was sometimes a pretend presidential candidate.

"So only lead we got is to follow Splater, see who the American is, go from there?"

"Roger that."

He looked at his watch.

"Give me a couple of minutes to make sure we've got a tail on Splater. Feel like a meal?"

"Sure. Do your call and I'll order up some Spätzle and Bratwurst."

"Oh, I love those." He smiled. "Any desert?"

She finally smiled back, hands on her hips. "Of course. Why do you think I'm ordering it up here? Can't send you back horny."

December 15, 2011; New York City, NY, Manhattan

Zack's FBI team tailing Splater had followed his car to the airport.

They quickly identified the passenger he picked up as Kent Mantribe, a honcho Republican lobbyist.

As they approached the West 79th Street Boat Basin, the team exchanged a look.

One spoke into a phone. "Keep the drone on them, they are going by water. We'll head back there to monitor."

They'd snapped dozens of photos of the airport pickup and the boarding of the boat.

Since they didn't have a boat, they'd have to be satisfied with drone surveillance.

Over an Hour Later; 20 Miles East of Long Island

The boat carrying Splater and Mantribe pulled up beside the big yacht. They boarded Antony Sopranov's luxury yacht and walked into his personal quarters.

Sopranov walked out to greet them with two scantily dressed women.

"Put your coats on girls, you're getting on the other boat for a while," he said, swatting the ass of the nearest girl.

To Mantribe and Splater, he said, "When we're done, we'll have them back over and you can enjoy them."

The men smiled.

"Please, sit down. What are you drinking?"

* * * *

The men ate lobster and drank great wine.

"Will Obama be re-elected?" Sopranov asked Mantribe.

"Most likely, but it'll be a helluva race."

"Who will Republicans run? Will the new Tea Party run a candidate?" Splater asked.

* * * *

They talked at length of their friend, New York developer Dale Woody, his popularity, and his ability to give voice to the forgotten in America.

"For a rich playboy, his celebrity insulates him from character attacks," Splater observed.

"Woody is what he is," Mantribe said. "He knows two things: don't sweat the small stuff, and it's all small stuff."

They laughed importantly. Woody had already declined to seek the 2012 Republican nomination.

"Dale told me," Splater confided, "If Romney gets elected, that'd be fine by him; and if Obama were elected, Dale will keep his hat in the ring by sniping at Obama from the sidelines with high profile bullshit."

"Your country never gets good candidates," Sopranov smiled. "You can't have Tutin; now he's a thoroughbred."

"Kent, can you get Dale to run in 2016?" Splater asked.

"Don't know. He can't win the Republican nomination, or the general. What would he get out of it?"

Sopranov smiled a knowing smile, locked his fingers together on the edge of the table, and twirled his thumbs for a while.

Finally he spoke.

"Well. Woody is a businessman. We are businessmen. It is all about bottom line," he shrugged charmingly.

Mantribe cocked his head. Sopranov was right. Woody

would do anything for the right price.

"You did so good with Tumultus," Sopranov continued. "We want to expand on that. Bigly. You're our guy. Double the price."

Mantribe's mouth gaped open.

"What are you asking of me, exactly?"

"Can we help defeat Obama next November?"

"My guess is he gets reelected next year. If you want to get into it, though, I can come up with a plan for you."

Palm up, Sopranov said softly, "That is what I ask, exactly."

"Is Dale part of that plan?" Splater interjected.

"Hey, it's our plan," Mantribe shrugged. "I'd love it if our own thoroughbred made the race."

"Felix will organize payment to you," Sopranov said, closing down the conversation. "Start planning. Have something preliminary soon and come see me in Moscow."

They shook hands.

* * * *

That night, Zack answered his phone on the plane.

The voice on the phone, an agent who'd followed Splater and Mantribe, said, "Sorry we couldn't get sound, Zack. But we did get pictures. Plus we identified the American."

"Shit. But good job."

Zack hung up. He pursed his lips. Why the hell was a Russian mob front man meeting with a honcho lobbyist and Tutin's banker friend, who laundered the Russian mob's money?

Why didn't the damn drone grab sound, too?

Early 2012; Moscow, Russia

Mantribe proved why he was a legendary campaign honcho and lobbyist.

Sopranov led him through a blitz of meetings with Russians, including a cyber team, other oligarchs, and President Tutin himself.

At each meeting, Mantribe began, "Here is a plan for 2016. *Operation Insurrection*. There are two basic parts."

Following week; Moscow, Russia

Pierre Montesquieu, an agent for the French General Directorate for External Security in Russia, waited patiently for Jules.

He almost preferred to meet her publicly, so she'd kiss him and snuggle up to him to hear what he had to say.

He caught her slim figure approaching. He waved.

She hugged and kissed him.

Arms around each other, they went for a walk, covertly looking all around while seeming to have eyes only for each other.

He punched a button on his phone and whispered in her ear, "Know who Kent Mantribe is?"

"Yes."

"He was here last week."

It was a little unusual for her NOT to know about a high profile American in Moscow.

"Why?"

A Russian man walked close to them and they stopped talking. Pierre turned her face to him and they kissed.

Jules opened her eyes to see if the Russian was still there. He'd moved on.

Jules and Pierre walked further away before speaking

again.

"Sopranov took him to a series of meetings with Russians – cyber geeks, oligarchs, and even Tutin."

"Who hired him?"

"Guess Sopranov. They talked about an election."

"The U.S. election this year?"

"I don't know. But that's my guess. You know Steve Champion?"

"Know of him, never met him."

"Here we go," he stopped at a car and opened the front door for her. "Say hey to Champ."

She shook his hand smiling, "So you're the legend."

* * * *

The three of them sat at a picnic table at the edge of a large park.

"Mantribe has been running an influence campaign in Europe and the U.S. to gin up support for Russia in the political realm for years now," Champion began.

Steve Champion, a former officer with MI6, the U.K.'s foreign intelligence service, uncovered a giant operation against Britain not long after arriving in Moscow a decade ago, and was promptly chased out, his cover blown.

Champion turned his considerable talents to creating his London-based company, Kuklos Intelligence. Kuklos means "circle" in Greek.

"When did it start – what's the goal?"

"Far as I can tell, it started in or around 2006. Mantribe's been on Tutin's – Sopranov's – payroll since 2007. Mantribe's pulled in nearly $50 million in consulting fees between 2007 and 2010 from Russia alone."

"He's moved most of his money offshore now, generally the Caymans and Switzerland."

"The goal?"

"Our guess is an influence campaign. God knows your country is susceptible. With the advent of your Fox News, fake news finds a home with the Americans."

"A minority of Americans – and not *my* Fox News."

"Nevertheless, a significant and growing number of your countrymen believe the bullshit these guys are manipulating them with."

She looked at him unhappily.

"When were you there last, love?" Pierre asked.

"A while," she said looking away, suddenly homesick but glad she wasn't there right now, either.

March 8, 2012; Moscow, Russia, Kremlin, Tutin's Office

Newly elected for another term, despite the American's attempt to diminish him in Russia, Vadik Tutin met with his old friend, Nikolay Orlov.

Orlov walked into the ornate office.

"Today, I turn page on intelligence in Russia," Tutin said, hands on his hips. Orlov knew his old friend would not have come to this place lightly. Tutin was a creation of the old KGB.

"Best way to sideline NATO is to marginalize U.S. We may not change who U.S. voters pick, but I want to try to manipulate them. Take the fight to cyberspace and fuck with their elections."

"That is great!" Orlov said, relishing the moment when the president was finally agreeing with him. He'd been lobbying Tutin to do exactly this.

"I meet next with new head of military intelligence," Tutin confided. "I am ordering him to repurpose our psychological operations from use in war zones to use for elections."

Orlov smiled broadly. "We can leverage that greatly with social media. I want to build massive troll farms, botnet spamming operations and fake news outlets for wider dissemination – or what Americans call 'rat fucking' in elections."

"I like that, 'rat fucking.' Bot-what? Troll farms?"

Mid-November, 2012; Washington, D.C., Mantribe's Office

Mantribe glanced at the *Washington Post* headline: *"Obama Prepares for Second Inaugural."*

Watching the disastrous campaign and presidential election unfold in 2012, Mantribe took notice of every mistake.

He picked up his phone, stopped on the contact "Dash Rock," and called.

Miami, Florida; Home of Dash Rock

His colorful name was often a metaphor for Dash Rock's political rise. He rose meteorically fast – because he was so tough. There was nothing he wouldn't do to win an election.

His Hollywood good looks and ease on camera only enhanced his reputation.

Sitting by his pool reading the *Wall Street Journal*, Dash picked up the phone on the second ring.

"Kent, always good to hear from you."

"Time for a visit, my friend. Any chance you can come sit with me soon?"

The notorious attorney Roy Cohn introduced Rock to Dale Woody, a brash New York realtor, in 1979.

When Rock and Mantribe founded a lobbying practice the following year, Woody became one of their first clients.

By the late 1980s, Rock and Mantribe were two of Woody's closest advisors, and favorite friends.

Rock moved to Miami to invest in real estate and dabble in local and national Republican campaigns, with side gigs as a cable political commentator.

Rock even served as chairman of Woody's 2000 presidential exploratory advisory committee. He'd waited way over a decade now to get a chance to race that horse.

November 29, 2012; Washington, D.C., Mantribe's Office

Rock sat across from his old friend in Mantribe's Capitol-view office.

"So, what are you doing January 20?" Rock asked, laying a paper on Mantribe's desk detailing Obama's January 20 inauguration, which disgusted both men.

"I propose we get ready for 2016. Listen to what I'm up to; I need you in it with me."

* * * *

Several hours later, the old friends and partners shook hands at the door of Mantribe's office.

"See you in Miami in January. Stay the whole week. You need some color."

Rock winked and left.

Mantribe closed the door and pumped his fist, nodding, he walked back to his desk. This was a gargantuan task. But getting Dash onboard would make the journey easier. And more fun.

Dash was a player, and a pro.

BOOTS AND BOTS

March 2, 2013; near St. Petersburg, Russia, Black Sea Dock

After flying to St. Petersburg with the ambassador, Jules got off the plane in disguise and drove to the tiny boat dock.

"Ahoy, love," Pierre greeted her.

"Hey, gawd, it stinks here," she said.

"Fish trash and pollution, easier ride is five minutes out."

She stuck her arms in the bands on the side of the zodiac and held on for a herky-jerky ride to the midsize boat Pierre procured for them.

Just off Helsinki, Finland

The luxury yacht flying a French flag was anchored a few miles off Helsinki. Pierre's smaller boat approached it from behind.

The French agents who met them, greeted Pierre fondly; he introduced them to Jules.

"We'll drydock your boat back here," one said. "They're upstairs."

* * * *

Jules and Pierre entered a room with Steve Champion and Zack.

"Zack!" Jules sounded genuinely pleased. She pranced

over to him and grabbed him in a big hug. They kissed.

"Hey Champ," she said, pulling away, shaking Champion's hand.

"You kiss everybody but me," he fake pouted.

She grabbed his face, pulling him in for a wet, over-the-top kiss.

She pulled away. "Happy?"

"Ye- … yes. Yes. I mean, thank you. My, my," he stumbled. Very British.

* * * *

Seated around a table with desert in front of them, Zack said, "Let me play this for you. We picked this up in New York."

He was covering Jules' tapping of the phone, although they both trusted these guys.

"Sopranov never makes his own calls," said Zack.

"It was recorded 13 December, 2011 Sopranov to Splater, a New York Russian mob guy," said Jules.

Zack clicked on the screen in front of him.

"Our American friend from Tumultus – set up meeting with him, please. Where we were before. You know time and day, right?"

Pierre and Steve exchanged a knowing look.

"That's all there was from him. He hung up," said Jules.

Zack hit the clicker. The screen lit up with photos of Splater's surveillance, airport pickup, getting on the boat at the dock, and drone footage.

"My team got on Splater. He picked up Kent Mantribe, got in a boat and drove into the ocean for 20 miles, hooked up with Sopranov on board his yacht."

The pictures taken by the drone included dozens of

shots of happy laughing, earnest talking, and liaisons with prostitutes for all three men.

"So, turns out we're all interested in Mantribe," said Pierre.

"You know what Tumultus is," said Champion matter-of-factly.

"Do you?" said Jules.

"It was an influence operation out of Russia, starting in 2006-ish, aimed at Europe and the United States," Champion said. "It was entirely a data-mining, influence campaign."

"Is it commercial, political, governmental?" asked Zack.

"If Russia is doing it, it is entirely political, manipulative," Pierre mumbled.

"To what end?" asked Zack.

"Power," Champion said.

"Always," said Jules. "But this time, what's the specific goal? We're missing something."

She smiled and imitated a captain in a classic movie. "Russians don't take a dump without a plan, son."

"To undermine NATO, and western democracies?" Champion guessed. "Unclear."

* * * *

Zack punched up a graphic of money being moved — and businesses created — in both the Caymans and in Switzerland.

"We've got tons of money originating in Russia going into the Caymans and Switzerland," he said. "Separately, we've got tons of newly active businesses and public interest organizations taking an active interest in Republican politics created in one of those two places."

Now Zack's presentation on the screen on the wall showed websites of several of the more radical right wing faux news sites, including CNS News, Media Research Center, Universal Free Press, Independent Journalism Review, World Truth TV, Western Center for Journalism, World Net Daily/WND, News Max, The Federalist (and the Federalist Papers), Freedom Works, The Political Insider, Heartland Institute, Patriot Journal, Freedom Daily, and the Washington Examiner.

"This spike of new businesses and fake public interest sites created behind the offshore banking curtain are buying millions of dollars' worth of ads on the alt-right wing echo chamber," Zack continued.

"Fox, Breitbart, Infowars, hundreds of bloggers … are all promoting fake news sites, and fake reports about official sounding stuff – fake polls, data mining. They did that in Britain," Champion said.

"Social media quizzes people take about their favorite color or guess their birth year or their IQ … majority of those these days are Russian-generated," Pierre said. "All to figure out who is susceptible to certain predispositions or ideas."

"Then they reach out in those terms to promote their message, their candidate, whatever," Zack finished.

"So the Russians have weaponized information beyond the former Soviet Republics," Jules said slowly, looking overwhelmed.

"We are so susceptible," Zack winced. "Fox News was born to get Congress to impeach a president for lying about a blow job."

"And nipple licking. You read the report then, right?"

"Wasn't even good porn. Ask your lover," said Pierre, smiling wickedly and gesturing to Zack.

Champion looked down.

Zack looked at Pierre, then Jules.

Jules smiled, looking at Pierre unbelievingly.

"Friends," she smiled, explaining with one hand chopping the other. "With benefits." Smirking, she said, "I'm appalled the Frenchman didn't catch that nuance."

"I don't need to know that," Champion said.

They laughed.

* * * *

"The Supreme Court made it much harder for us to follow the money in politics since 2010," Zack said.

"*Citizens United,*" said Jules, the Court decision that invalidated nearly all laws related to campaign finance, "Was either monumental stupidity or colossal naiveté. In that decision, the court said politics would police itself."

Zack humphed, "FBI can't even police the crimes going on *near* political stuff. What we're getting great at is tracing money. But since nobody has to report that anymore, it's often a dead end."

"Russians aren't putting money where you can find it," Pierre said.

"No kidding," Zack said. "It's flowing through hundreds of shells, money washed through dozens of international banks."

"The Brits can help you in the Caymans," Champion said.

"We can help you in Switzerland," Pierre said. "This is, how you say in United States, our second rodeo."

"Meaning Tumultus?" Jules asked, hand on the table.

"Yes," Champion said.

As an aside to Pierre, Jules touched his arm, "The particular smart ass idiom you are looking for is: 'this ain't our first rodeo.'"

"Thanks, love," Pierre smiled at Jules. "In 2009, by the time we discovered the scope and intentions, we did a British-French operation on private banking actions."

"We stole banking information and data to prove we weren't just guessing, but since we stole the proof; we can't use it," Champion said.

"So how can we prosecute?" Zack asked, knowing full well the laws of his country – or any democracy – were ill-suited to proving this level of infiltration.

March 10, 2013; Sochi, Russia, Tutin's Seaside Villa

Mantribe and Rock arrived with Splater.

The entire cabal – minus the president – was waiting in the giant library, a fireplace on each side of the room.

It offered a spectacular view of the Black Sea's wild, constant spray against the rocky shore.

A giant storm was brewing.

These were the men who were closest to the president. They had trusted each other with their lives many times over. This cabal was an unbreakable partnership.

The trio from the United States was greeted first by Sopranov, who'd grown up with the President and largely financed many of his nefarious schemes over the years.

Sopranov embraced all three men.

Then he led all three to each of the players.

"You may know Stepan Kozlov," said Sopranov.

"Mr. Ambassador, always an honor," said Mantribe.

"Good to see you, Kent," Kozlov said.

"How's your poker game, Stepan?" asked Rock.

"We'll have to go back to Las Vegas for you to see that, Dash," Kozlov smiled.

Stepan Kozlov, the Russian Ambassador to the United States, looked older than he was, although that was because he was grossly overfed.

He was a perfect ambassador for Tutin: gregarious, popular, always in the know about Washington – and true blue, former KGB.

Mantribe and Rock – both clothes horses – had each noticed Kozlov was wearing the same blue suit he always wore. His shirt was just a little too tight around his neck under his round, pleasant face.

Kozlov met Tutin studying law at Saint Petersburg State University. When they graduated in 1975, for lack of better job options, they both joined the KGB. Kozlov was posted to the U.S.; Tutin to East Germany.

Good friends, the two couldn't be more different, personality-wise. Kozlov was scholarly and affable; Tutin was socially awkward, more schooled in the real politic matters of state – which probably explained their KGB postings. And current jobs.

* * * *

Outside in the howling wind, two figures were holding cameras especially made for filming distances. Dressed in black and standing behind a giant rock, they fought the increasing wind, struggling to hold their cameras steady.

"Gawd, this place is so fucking cold," said Jules, shivering.

Pierre agreed. Looking at the sky, he asked, "Where's your chief?"

The U.S. spy chief was Moscow's senior western spy, and usually sniffed out the most perilous matters.

"He's running down something else, in St. Pete, and the spy academy," she yelled over the loud wind. "Didn't say more."

Spies for NATO nations and other democracies

worked closely together in Moscow. Figuring out Russia's intentions took the resources of more than any single nation.

* * * *

Rapid lightening flashed outside the large windows.

"This is Nikolay Orlov, director of the Russian Institute for Strategic Studies," Sopranov continued with the introductions.

"Dr. Orlov, it's good to see you again," Mantribe gushed. "Dash, this guy is scary smart. He was an early pioneer here in electronic communications."

"Oh … bots?" asked Rock.

Mantribe nodded enthusiastically.

Nikolay Orlov rose to Lieutenant General during a 33-year-career in Russia's foreign intelligence service. His institute housed the largest, most advanced cyber hacking unit in the world.

As the Berlin Wall fell on November 9, 1989, he was out drinking with Tutin when they were called urgently back to the embassy.

Understanding the fast moving danger of an overthrow, the Russian ambassador to Germany, Orlov, and Tutin burned the embassy's KGB files to keep demonstrators from getting to them.

Orlov was a natural at understanding the breadth of uses of electronic communications, soon leading the world in perfecting the art of breaking into them and stealing data in the late 1990s/early 2000s.

The last five people in the room included Orlov's top deputy on his cyber team, three other oligarchs, and Tutin's top military spy.

Finally, Tutin entered.

"Mr. President!" Sopranov greeted him with a hug.

"Antony," the president said affectionately; he saw Mantribe. "Kent, I'm glad you are doing this with us, thank you for your help again."

"My honor, Mr. President."

"This is Dash Rock, a very tough U.S. political operator," Sopranov said.

"Yes, I have seen you on TV. You are good," the Russian president smiled.

* * * *

Outside, the high wind blew Jules down. There was a downside to being a little bitty thing. She rolled several feet before grabbing the limb of a tree and pulling herself to the tree trunk.

She pulled a rope from around her waist and ran it around the trunk. Attached to her body harness, she was locked on, and still battered by the wind.

* * * *

Gathered around the large oak table in the library, littered with drinks, plates and documents, the two Americans had the Russians' undivided attention as the storm raged outside.

"We're calling this *Operation Insurrection*," Mantribe began. "There are two major components: boots and bots."

"The bots are going to be entirely in your shop here, Nikolay, it's a full frontal cyber assault," Rock chimed in. "That's our air war. Unseen and deadly."

Rock, ever the dramatic grand strategist, deliberately put political matters in terms of war. Dash Rock was always at war, and he was always a Republican general.

With the Cold War so long ago, Rock sensed an opportunity for a relationship, and he knew Dale Woody shared that thinking.

"The cyber hacking starts as soon as possible," Mantribe picked up. "U.S. elections are virtually impossible to hack into. Fifty states, hundreds, sometimes thousands of local jurisdictions in each state, all responsible for vote counting, some by hand, many by machine. Many more ballots are counted by machine, but they are not networked."

"Nikolay, please explain quickly in Russian what that means – why we can't do this by hacking only."

Nikolay Orlov spoke quickly in Russian and gestured to Mantribe.

"Dash and I have taken a pretty comprehensive look at all 50 states, in terms of computer security, and none of it is that great – but it is secured."

"We can always break in," grinned Orlov arrogantly.

"We will count on that," said Mantribe.

"What *is* the least secure, and frequently shared with campaigns, is the voter databases in all 50 states," Rock confided.

Orlov smiled even bigger, looking so happy.

"Here's how that can work," said Rock. "We hack into individual voter databases, registering phantom voters by mail, using area addresses. If we can manipulate vote totals, that's great. But we mustn't count on that."

Thunder boomed outside.

"Here's our most audacious element … boots on the ground, the only part of this invasion force that will be visible, and the only part of this insurrection that can be vulnerable," Mantribe said.

"Our side has done an excellent job of injecting the

notion of illegal voting in the U.S. among blacks and Hispanics – that's who everybody's watching when they register," Rock added.

Mantribe paused before he spoke. "You have a number of – assets …"

Tutin looked bemused.

"Who can coordinate other associates and their family members, particularly older women into –"

"Wait," said Tutin, tapping his finger, thinking something through. "No. Key to success is keeping boots part secret, no?"

"Correct," Rock confirmed.

"How big is insurrection force?"

"One thousand –" Mantribe said.

"Five thousand," Rock interjected. Mantribe looked annoyed at him.

"Politics in the U.S. is entirely about math." Rock looked directly at Tutin. "The more people you can send, the more we can leverage votes in four strategic states –"

"All states that a Democrat needs to win to get to a victory in our electoral college," Mantribe added.

"I do not understand this particular institution of yours," said one of the other oligarchs in the room.

A sky full of zigzagging lightning lit up the room, causing a couple of these important men to look up with concern.

"It's just – ancient – in our constitution," Rock shrugged.

"We never changed it, so it's how we elect presidents," Mantribe said. "Our party doesn't want to change it – it has elevated Republicans over Democrats who got more popular votes several times when elections were close."

"Like George Bush," Tutin offered helpfully.

"Exactly," said Rock.

* * * *

Outside, the tree to which Jules was tied bent low in the wind, made a god-awful noise. She reached down to unlatch herself at the same moment the tree split, pulling Jules with it.

Pierre raced after her.

* * * *

"Our guys start registering as voters in Florida, Pennsylvania, Wisconsin and Michigan – yesterday," Mantribe said. "This requires having rental property, a believable story about a job they travel for, utilities in that name, and an ID that shows they live in that jurisdiction."

"They do this in jurisdiction after jurisdiction in these states only," Rock added. "The goal is to have each 'boot' registered in dozens of places in each state."

Splater finally spoke, "We will manage documents and records on boat in international waters off New York."

"Our first measure of success will be in the primaries," Rock said. "We will weaken the hell out of Clanton just doing that alone. And of course, we strengthen our preferred candidate in the Republican primary."

"A realtor, maybe?" joked another oligarch.

"Damn straight," smiled Splater.

"While those are the biggest parts of the strategy, there are others, expanding on what we've already been doing with Tumultus," Mantribe continued. "Party donations to Republicans in Congress, energy guys, chamber guys, gun guys, anti-abortion guys, and conservative causes through PACs registered offshore with dark money."

Gesturing to the other oligarchs in the room, Sopranov said, "We have already set up hundreds of businesses and accounts in Switzerland, the Caymans – to hide and provide the money for our boots."

Rock gestured back at Sopranov, "That level of commitment and low profile will mean all the difference in our success here."

"That kind of money also means we can run tons of outrageous ads in general from now forward," Mantribe added. "Traditionally, our party runs those from August through November. Now, we can do that anytime we want."

"Social media – and our courts – have made that much easier," Rock noted.

"Yes," said Nikolay Orlov. "We are growing farms of people to circulate our messages – troll farms. We will hack into email servers of political parties, and private servers for people on campaigns."

"We have a route to release through WikiLeaks; Assange hates Clanton, too," Orlov continued. "We will edit a few select emails to add information that implicates candidates in whatever could hurt them."

He fist bumped with Rock.

"We will have months of stories about whatever is actually *in* emails we hack, plus the things we will stick in emails – those will be the most fun – and our trolls will spread those with impunity," Mantribe said.

"Last, and this is strictly from my dirty tricks handbook, and for Felix and I to deal with over there, is some last minute Election Day tomfoolery in swing states," Rock explained.

"That'll reduce Democratic turnout and fuck with ballots after they are stored in election offices to prevent any kind of recount, if it were close enough to go there."

Mantribe held up his hands. "That's it."

"Is very good," Tutin smiled.

"Who will you make win?" asked an oligarch.

"We begin this with no chance of knowing who wins – or who's gonna make it to the show, um, the general election. Two sets of 50 primaries, another 50 state elections," said Mantribe. "What we've done is guarantee that if Hailey Clanton wins, it will be with so much baggage, that she will be even more ineffective than Obama is."

Tutin's eyes narrowed.

Noticing that, Rock spoke up. "We guarantee by the end of the campaign – whoever is elected – Russia wins."

* * * *

Still buffeted by gale force winds, Jules' sat on a rock beside a tree. Pierre was sitting beside her, his body pushing her into a tree trunk, stabilizing them in the wind.

Her barely visible face showed a scrape from her struggle with the tree that broke with her attached to it earlier. It also broke a rib.

Suddenly, she pushed her finger into her ear.

"I think the drone might have crashed. Whatever happened, it stopped transmitting altogether. We're not getting shit out of this. Damnit!"

"We're still getting pictures."

* * * *

Sopranov walked the president to the library door, their heads together, talking animated.

"Good night," they hugged.

Tutin was headed to bed, by way of a mistress in the room next to his.

The other oligarchs headed out too, as well as Tutin's

top spy.

Sopranov swaggered back over to those remaining in the room: Mantribe, Rock, Splater, Ambassador Kozlov and Nikolay Orlov.

"Another round of brandy, my friends. This is group of men who will change the world."

He slugged the last of his brandy before pouring more.

"The president will send insurrection force of 4,000," he shrugged. "I know you asked for five, but he thinks that invites more scrutiny. I don't know. Or care."

Sopranov shot a look at Mantribe. "If that is not enough, say so now. I can revisit with him."

"No, that's plenty," Mantribe smiled.

"We can make documents for as many IDs as we need," said Splater. "If each one votes 25 times, that's 100,000 votes. We are confident that, with our voter depression efforts in target states, that might be enough to swing election. Either way, it will weaken Clanton."

"This may seem a strange question," Ambassador Kozlov asked. "How much do we tell Dale? Anything?"

"We don't tell him shit," Rock said. "Ever. Here's another American political term, 'plausible deniability.' Means the guy elected has to be insulated from this kinda detail stuff. If we don't tell him, he can say he doesn't know. Works better in the end."

"Agreed," smiled Orlov. "He tweets too much."

FIRST BLOOD

The next morning, Tutin, Nikolay Orlov, and Sopranov sat in the sauna room naked, barely visible through the waves of steam.

"I want all kinds of people for insurrection boots," Tutin said. "Dash said old women would be best. Maybe retired KGB?"

"Nah, we should just use disguises. Older people need doctors. Simpler is better," Sopranov said.

"Let's send them this summer," said Nikolay Orlov. "Puts them in U.S. for over three years. Good training for agents. Work will be easy. Nobody looks for us there."

"Carefully structure the units," Tutin said to Orlov. "I want us to know what is going on all the time. No contact with our other spies there. Nothing to invite suspicion."

"Understood."

Sopranov wiped his face. "Kent and Dash agree – tell Woody nothing."

"Thank God," Tutin said, relieved, as the towel boy walked in with robes and frozen vodka. "This is best for us. I like Woody. But he is just our useful fool."

March 12, 2013; Shchelkovo, Russia, Spy Training Academy

Twenty miles northeast of downtown Moscow, Nikolay Orlov and a uniformed Russian general walked into the ornate administration building on the campus of Russia's elite spy training academy.

* * * *

The two men, sitting at a desk with a third man, the administrator, also in a Russian uniform, spoke rapidly.

"How quickly can you jump up the cadet population?" Nikolay Orlov asked.

"Must be very best," said the general who had come in with Orlov.

"We have just under 10,000 training at various facilities," said the administrator. "How many do you need for your 'boots'?"

"Need 4,000," said Nikolay Orlov. "So bring many more than that. We'll winnow them down from here."

March 20, 2013; Shchelkovo, Russia, Spy Training Academy

Nikolay Orlov and the Russian Academy administrator watched fresh faced young Russians step on the mark on the floor while a special camera whizzed through dozens of detailed shots, of their faces, head and upper body.

"We have 5,000 students here now, all our top prospects," the administrator said. "Cameras are sending images to mask makers so we have consistent look for the various IDs."

He cut his eyes at Orlov. "Is good plan," he nodded admiringly.

"Who's teaching U.S. voting 101?" Orlov smiled back.

April 26, 2013; Moscow, Russia, Just off Red Square

Jules and her immediate boss, the CIA chief of station, were having a rare public meeting. Like most of her meetings she most wanted to cover up, she pretended it was a love affair.

They walked along a busy street of markets with outdoor seating for the midday lunch crowd.

Arm in arm, she laid her head on his arm while he whispered in her ear. With the whiteout app on, keeping their conversation just beyond electronic surveillance, he said, "They are moving in tons of spy cadets to their academy – there's so much activity there, that-"

The spray of blood on Jules' face came from nowhere.

She never heard the shot.

She drew her gun and struggled to pull her chief into a doorway for cover as his body crumbled.

Across the street, the station chief's driver ran to them, gun drawn. He was startled by the amount of blood on both of them.

"Where's the car?" Jules yelled, pulling one of the chief's arms over her shoulder; the driver did the same, pointing at the car.

The Americans ran for it.

Russians on the street looked at them curiously, then with greater concern when they saw the blood.

Jules got in the back seat, hauling the chief in with her. The driver shoved the chief's lower body in and slammed the door. He jumped in front and tore off.

Jules got her first good look at her friend and station chief. His eyes were open and dead. A hole the size of a quarter showed where the bullet exited in his lower neck. The blood flow had slowed considerably, but then his heart had stopped beating.

"No," Jules moaned. "Gawd, no," she whispered, cradling his head gently.

"Which hospital?"

Teary, she shook her head at him. "Embassy morgue," she whispered, looking around. "If we're not being chased, don't speed."

April 29, 2013; Shchelkovo, Russia, Spy Training Academy

On the proving ground, thousands of cadets went through the careful daily routine of a morning exercise. Over half were women.

Nikolay Orlov and the Russian Academy administrator watched from a tower near the edge of the field.

"We are well organized; 200 teams," the administrator told Nikolay Orlov. "Each team of 20 has a leader and proctors familiar with U.S. customs and protocols."

"Biggest part of their training will come on site, just waiting and blending into the United States," the administrator continued. "Voting is easy part. Do you worry we are sending them too early?"

"No," Orlov said. "We have an accelerated calendar."

May 16, 2013, Booz Allen office, Kunia Camp, Hawaii, U.S.

Edward Snowden – an IT specialist who'd moved up the ladder quickly with a reputation as a genius who could fix, find flaws with, or build anything electronic – sat at his desk in the golden morning sun.

With the computer screen reflecting in his square-rimmed glasses, Snowden downloaded information onto a large external hard drive, changing it out frequently, filling dozens of drives.

His boss walked into Snowden's office. "Hey, boss."

"I didn't know you had epilepsy, Ed. What kind of treatment are you getting in Portland?" his boss asked.

Snowden looked uncomfortable. "Yeah, that's why I had to leave Special Forces," he lied. "I whacked my head in training, gave me epilepsy. There's a new therapy I'm a candidate for. Trial's in Portland."

"No problem with the time off. I'm out tomorrow,

back the week you are gone."

* * * *

Around noon, a colleague stuck her head in the door. "Want me to bring you something for lunch?"

"Nah, I'm headed out in a few. Hey, I need to check your dedicated laptop; looks like somebody's binging it, trying to tap in."

Dedicated laptops had no public internet connection and no external drives to download materials.

"There a breech?"

"Nope, just staying ahead of it," Snowden said earnestly.

"Stay far ahead, dude. Mahalo," she thanked him in Hawaiian.

Snowden walked to her office, closed and unplugged the laptop – then wrote a note: "Haven't figured what's up with laptop. Not certain secure. If you need it, it's in the vault."

Back in his office, Snowden put the laptop in the vault with several others with the same secure markings.

He left for lunch with a backpack full of high volume hard drives.

Snowden's Home; Kunia Camp, Hawaii

That night, Snowden methodically unscrewed the backs of the dedicated laptops, removing drives and hooking them up to a copying device.

May 20, 2013; Kunia Camp, Hawaii, Snowden's bedroom

Snowden pushed a dedicated laptop into the carry-on

bag on top of his bed, along with three others there. He zipped up the bag.

"Honey, are you ready?" His girlfriend called from the other room.

He walked out.

Honolulu, Hawaii; International Airport, Curbside Drop off

Snowden stepped up to check his big bag at the curb, his girlfriend waiting to hug him goodbye. He handed his ticket and passport to the agent.

"To Hong Kong today, sir?"

"Hong Kong – I thought you were going to Portland," his girlfriend said, surprised.

"Two days in Hong Kong for business, then Portland. Just found out."

"All set," the agent said, handing Snowden his passport and bag tag.

"See you next week," he lied, getting in his last hug.

May 22, 2013; Kunia Camp, Hawaii, Booz Allen office

The colleague whose dedicated laptop Snowden had copied wandered into Snowden's office.

She went to the vault to retrieve her laptop, laying her hand on the pad beside the vault, watching it scan her palm, hearing it snap open.

A male colleague walked in. "Oh, while you've got that open, let me get my laptop out. Snowden was doing …."

The woman narrowed her eyes and opened the vault wider until they could see a half dozen of the hardened laptops inside.

"What the …" she muttered.

The man reached in to pull out the laptop on top, and

a screw fell out of the bottom of it.

"Shit, this has been fiddled with," he said.

"Probably Snowden, though. I mean that's his job," she said.

"Yeah. Let me check something." He opened the laptop and typed in a string of code.

He blanched and turned the screen to her. It read, "HARD DRIVE COPIED 16MAY 2013, 1155 PM."

"Call Snowden now," she said.

"He's supposed to be in Portland."

She sat at Snowden's station and said, "Let's see if TSA checked him." She tapped the keys.

"Fuck. He arrived in Hong Kong yesterday."

The two looked at each other blinking, not believing that their relatively new employee could be a bad guy.

"What's the protocol?" he asked quietly.

"You go lock the place down, I'll call the FBI," she said. "Meet me back here, we'll call the boss."

May 28, 2013; Washington, D.C., FBI Director's office

Behind the door labeled "Director of the Federal Bureau of Investigation," a concerned voice said, "Who the hell is Edward Snowden? How bad is it?"

"Stunningly bad, sir," said a second voice.

June 6, 2013

The *Guardian* newspaper in London, England, ran the first story based on Snowden's cache of American secrets, this one on the megadata gathering program.

"Megadata" is the log of all electronic traffic flowing through U.S. communication companies, including private and corporate emails, texts, postings — any consumer electronic footprint.

That data was available to U.S. investigators with a warrant from the FISA court, which triggered a notification to Congress.

The U.S. had learned in the wake of 9-11 that private companies had varying standards for retaining that data, and some companies didn't want to turn over data without a warrant. That cost the nation time and energy just to look at data related to the hijackers, setting back the investigation from the outset.

When Congress debated the law in 2001, most said they would not pass the megadata program if private records could be viewed by the government at will.

Requiring a warrant from the courts satisfied the concern over Fourth Amendment privacy needs. But in the intervening years, privacy advocates agitated against the collection or retention of any type of megadata.

So the *Guardian* story was scandalous. Insidious. Mischaracterized. But scandalous.

* * * *

Jules read the story that morning from her secure laptop, breathing heavily.

"I swear to gawd … if you get me killed, too, you dick," she muttered under her breath.

Shuddering, she flashed back to the moment a sticky spray of blood splattered on her face not so long ago.

She walked around the room with nervous energy.

June 14, 2013; New York City, FBI, Financial Crimes Unit

Jake Commings, the Financial Crimes Unit boss and prosecutor, knocked at Zack's open door.

"Hey boss."

Commings closed the door.

"What's up?" Zack asked

"Feel like a change of scenery?"

"Why?"

"I've been asked to succeed Robert Mueller as FBI Director," Commings said. "Come with me."

"You're on, sir."

Zack stood up and they shook hands. Cummings put his butt on Zack's desk.

"Seen this? Expect it will be on our plate for years."

He tossed a copy of the U.S. Department of Justice's charges against Snowden for two counts of violating the Espionage Act of 1917 and theft of government property.

"I knew this was coming. How bad is the breech?" He scanned the charging document.

"It's the worst ever, Zack."

Zack locked on his eyes. "Any chance he had access to overseas agents?"

Commings nodded, unhappy. "It wouldn't surprise me if we started seeing agents drop out of sight all over the place."

Zack flashed back to Jules, giving her a butt rub.

"We're gonna get on this before you get sworn in?"

"Yes. You go to D.C. tomorrow to head the Snowden Task Force."

June 19, 2013; Shchelkovo, Russia, Spy Training Academy

In the grand hall, it was graduation day for the all-important boots on the ground insurrection force that was entirely about weakening democracy in the United States.

Soon, the 4,000 Russian spies would depart for their

sojourn around the U.S. swing states of Florida, Pennsylvania, Michigan and Wisconsin.

President Tutin stepped forward to congratulate the graduates.

"The nature of war – and intelligence – has changed," he said. "Russia – and our intelligence agencies – are at the vanguard of this global change."

Proud faces cheered their leader, and themselves.

"History will remember you with awe and wonder. I envy you. You carry the hopes and dreams of a Greater Russia as you take our insurrection to American streets. Remember your training. Don't get caught."

He winked dramatically at the cadets, now officially agents of Russian State Security, the child of the old KGB.

Smiles shined from their faces.

He grabbed the podium, moving his face around so he was seen looking at each corner of the room.

"When you come home, find me. I want to hear all your stories."

The laughter of camaraderie echoed through the chamber.

"Congratulations on being the frontline of our insurrection. Go make us proud."

The standing ovation thundered on for several minutes, a former spy and their president, inspiring these present-day spies.

It was a great day for these young moles.

Their sendoff portended great peril for their longtime adversary, the United States.

June 21, 2013; Washington, D.C., FBI HQ, Secure Room

The incoming FBI Director, Jake Commings, and

Zack sat in a small room with three CIA briefers.

"After he dropped out of high school, Snowden enlisted in the Army Reserve in 2004 as a Special Forces candidate through a special enlistment recruiting computer geeks, but dropped out four days later," said the first briefer.

"Not cut out for the military life?" Zack asked sarcastically.

"Right, but he desperately wants to do something important," said the second briefer.

Zack did the uh-oh face, rolling his eyes.

"He gets a job as a security guard at the Maryland Language Institute, which is close to NSA," said the first briefer.

"Exaggerating the hell out of his four-day Special Forces training, he was in the computer department the next month, and being recruited by the NSA after that," said the second briefer.

Commings sat stoically mortified while Zack put his face in his hands.

"Snowden was part of a new phenomenon for us, a genius with no formal higher education, but a whiz at electronic communications. Everybody needs the geniuses; and we haven't cared if they really fit our culture of *protecting* secrets," the first briefer said candidly.

"That was a horrendous calculation on our part," Commings finally said to nods.

"By mid-2006, Snowden had worked at the NSA for a while before getting an IT job at CIA," the second briefer picked up. "Despite his lack of formal credentials, we gave him a top-secret clearance and posted him under State Department cover in Geneva."

Commings and Zack shook their heads at each other.

"In 2009, his CIA supervisor saw a distinct change in

his behavior … going off on anti-Obama rants at the office," the first briefer said. "We fired him the following week for trying to break into classified computers."

"FUCK," shouted Zack incredulously. "So the high school dropout who wants to be important gets a security clearance with access to our secrets from all over the world? He gets fired for trying to steal classified docs, and he NEVER LOSES HIS SECURITY CLEARANCE?"

"Look I didn't do it – we're as mortified as you are," the first briefer said evenly. "I got friends out there who might die from this."

"Me too," Zack whispered.

"All we can do is be painfully honest with you. The warnings from Geneva never got to the NSA, which re-hired him at a military facility in Japan," said the second briefer. "Early this year, he joined Booz Allen, even after their screeners found résumé discrepancies."

"Plus he bragged online that he joined Booz Allen to steal our top-secrets," said the first briefer.

"Let me just –" Incoming Director Commings was at a loss. "What is the status of Snowden's security clearance this minute?"

"Cancelled," said the second briefer.

"And his passport? He's still in Hong Kong, right?"

"Yeah, no place to go," Zack picked up with what he knew. "Passport's cancelled. But Hong Kong wants him out, if he can find a place to land."

Hong Kong, China, Hong Kong International Airport

Snowden and an international rights lawyer stood in the screening line for their Aeroflot flight to Moscow's Sheremetyevo Airport.

A Chinese official stood with them.

The official spoke to the screener, showing him a badge and a document.

Snowden stepped forward and presented his passport and ticket – and the screener stamped both, handing the documents back to Snowden.

Washington, D.C., FBI Headquarters, Secure Room

Commings and Zack were standing and shaking hands with the briefers.

The phone for first briefer buzzed. "Excuse me," he said, stepping away.

"Zack will be my guy here," Commings said.

"Shit," said the first briefer. "Thanks." He hung up.

"Snowden's leaving Hong Kong. Our eyes on him there just watched a local official escort him through screening and walk him and his lawyer to a Moscow flight. It departs in 20 minutes."

"Russia? Holy shit." Zack mumbled, then paced around for a few seconds before stopping in front of Commings.

"Boss, what if I went to Moscow, asked for their cooperation on this?"

Zack turned quickly to the briefers. "Who's your station chief there? Good guy?"

"Great guy," said the first briefer. "I'll set up a meeting for you."

THE SNOWDEN WINDFALL

June 21, 2013; Moscow, Russia, U.S. Embassy, Secure Room

"…worst breech the agency has ever-" Zack told the Ambassador as the door opened.

Jules walked in, "Sorry to be late – Zack! If I'd known you were here, I'd have run," she smiled, shaking his hand formally.

"You … you're the chief of station?" Zack smiled, surprised. He'd expected the station chief to arrange a meeting for he and Jules.

"A relatively recent promotion," she said absently, as she settled into a seat across from them.

"So, what brings you here, Zachary?"

"Mission from the Justice Department. Two things really–"

"Snowden?"

"Yes, both have to do with his spying."

He turned to the Ambassador. "Mr. Ambassador, we are going to ask the Soviets, um, Russians to refuse Snowden entry. They want our secrets. We want to throw a wrench in the gears, hold it up. We want Russia to own him with a Russian passport."

"How far do I go?"

"Well, I go with you, but all the way to threatening to ban energy tech transfers."

"That could work," Jules said. "Get our stuff back."

"Yeah. Other thing," his eyes bore in on Jules'.

"I'm here to tell the CIA's station chief that Snowden may well be carrying her name and names of our other agents here. Our allies' agents here. He took a shitload of CIA and military info, none of which was related to the *Guardian* stories about privacy this month."

Jules cocked her head at him, almost like she was warning him to shut up.

"Ms. Archer, this is urgent and dangerous. Hear what I am saying. Snowden may have already revealed your name and CIA status to the Russians. And your sources here. Your boss asked me to tell you the director is considering reshuffling agents abroad. I'm supposed to get your thoughts."

Jules, smirk on her face, placed her hands gently on the table, and then drew around with the tips of her fingers. She breathed evenly.

"Agent Tolliver, that's a shitty idea. My team has contacts here." Her voice got more passionate. "We don't fall back when Russia is coming after us."

She whacked the table loudly and stood up. "I'm not leaving unless ordered to. Then I'll be loud about it."

The Ambassador stood up. "You can take it from here. She's very stubborn."

"Yes she is, should I stop back in your office?" Zack asked. "How long before we can meet with counterparts to make our pleading?"

"Just come by." He nodded at Jules and bounded out.

She punched in a code on the door and it locked.

"Well, here we are, all locked up in a soundproof, hack proof room. Shame to waste it."

He dropped off his coat and loosened his tie.

She sashayed over to him and they shared a passionate kiss. She put a finger on his lips as he pulled up her skirt.

"Hang on. Do you want a briefing first? It's a good

one."

Kissing her neck, he said, "I propose we make this a quickie – and finish up after your briefing."

They loosened up each other's clothes. He pulled up her skirt, pulled down her panties, and sat her on the table.

She kicked off the panties while pushing down his pants and underwear.

He pushed into her fast and they humped loudly, then gasped and jerked hard together.

Breathing raggedly, they laughed and kissed.

"So, this the first time you did it in a SCIF?" [Sensitive Compartmented Information Facility]

She cocked her head and looked as though she was trying to remember.

"It's the first time in *this* one," she teased.

Zack rolled his eyes.

"OK, briefing," she said, squirming off the table, swatting his ass. "Scoot, let me get to the box."

She pressed a knot on the table and a computer screen popped up. She laid her palm on it to access her files.

Suddenly, Zack was looking at photographs of the March confab between the Russians and the American lobbyists at Tutin's private Sochi dacha.

Mantribe, Rock, and Splater arriving on the tarmac nearby. The trio arriving at the dacha.

"Looking all thick as thieves," she said softly, scrolling through the pics.

"So what are they stealing?"

"Haven't figured that out yet," she said. "Here's the little parts of conversation we managed to grab from far away by drone," she slid over a single page.

She bit her lip in disappointment. "But there was a giant storm, see the clouds when Mantribe and Rock landed? That hit with gusto, just as they got there."

He read the disparate words and phrases, and who said them.

STATIC …

Tutin: "Kent, I'm glad you are doing this with us, thank you for your help again."

Mantribe: "My honor, Mr. President."

Sopranov: "This is Dash Rock, a very"

STATIC …

Rock: "air war."

STATIC …

Mantribe: "insurrection that can be vulnerable."

STATIC …

Rock: "Politics in the U.S. is entirely about math. The more people-"

STATIC …

Oligarch: "A realtor, maybe?"

STATIC …

Rock: "That level of commitment and low profile will mean all the difference."

STATIC …

Rock: "Social media – and our courts – have only made that easier."

STATIC …

Mantribe: "That's it."

Tutin: "Is very good."

NEXT MORNING: Towel boy heard Tutin call Woody the "useful fool."

Jules watched him reading, a deep frown on his face.

"What you are looking at is every word we wrangled out of the recording before it crashed. Static bursts were four to 15 minutes long."

He was shaking his head, looking skeptical.

"Here's the difference between an FBI agent and a CIA agent," she purred. "FBI sees this, says there's no context. Could be self-important crosstalk at a social event."

He smiled and nodded at her.

"CIA agent thinks the context is two Americans, one of whom had been in Russia twice now – and this time," she pointed at a photo – "with the president of the country. Gathered with his closest friend, supporters, and financiers."

He blinked, cocked his head, trying to get his hands around – whatever this was.

"Also, the CIA can officially confirm for the FBI that Tutin himself just said this is at least his second time working with Mantribe. He'd do bad in jail – might could flip him, see what you can get."

"'Air war' could be a reference to political commercials," Zack shrugged.

"Maybe 'insurrection' is the name of a movie," Jules snarked.

"'Level of commitment' usually refers to money," he continued. "'Low profile' means you're up to something. Tutin really called Woody a useful fool?"

"*Polezni durak*," she imitated Tutin in Russian. "Yes. Useful for what?"

Zack flicked through the photos on the screen, looking thoughtful.

"Always the worst part of investigations," he said. "Taking all the threads, trying to re-weave the cloth. It never looks how you think it should."

She smiled at him and stroked his face.

"I forgot how hot you are when you are so focused."

He turned his chair toward her. She sat in his lap and they cuddled, both lost in thought.

"Every fiber of my being says these guys are up to something wicked, but I can't prove it in court," she said.

He slowly said, "It's time for you to get out."

She sat up and gave him a long, bemused look. "Zack Tolliver, I'm the chief of Moscow station. Time to go? What the fuck?"

"This just got much more dangerous. Snowden's going to have your name in his billions of files. Or – something that identifies you. You won't know when they figure it out."

He paused. "You'll just see the gun flash. We may or may not find your body."

"No need to scare me, sweetie," she said, laying her hand on his cheek gently.

Then she playfully slapped him.

"Zack, I'm trained for this. I'm dug in."

"When did you get promoted?" he asked, betting he knew. The U.S. was already missing another spy.

She rolled her eyes and looked away, stood up and walked to the other side of the table. "Right after the old chief was assassinated."

"That'd be exhibit one, why it's time to go."

She sat on the table, back to him.

"He was telling me the Russians were moving in several thousand more spy cadets to their academy near Moscow. That's unusual. They are very predicable with those type movements."

She blanched.

"Then a bullet came out of his neck and his blood squirted all over me."

Zack closed his eyes, stood up and walked around to stand beside her. He sat on the table beside her, gently rubbing the back of her hand gripping the table.

"That's the other thing with his murder. You don't kill the spies, you kick us out, bust our cover. They are *so* up to something they don't want us to sniff out."

* * * *

The next morning, back in the SCIF, with papers scattered on the table, Zack suddenly reached over and put his hand on hers.

"Look, I know you are the toughest motherfucker on the scene. But you are human, babe. Suppose they do catch on to you. How do you get out?"

"Oh, I've always got a back door and a way out," she said playfully.

"I don't wanna know your secrets … I'm just wondering if there's a way I can be helpful in extracting you if the time comes."

Her eyes narrowed as she debated in her head.

"If I'm ever running, I've got a couple of vehicles hidden away and will likely head for a plane, land someplace in the Caspian near the Azeri border."

She wrote down a number on a piece of paper. "Here's the transponder for the plane. If you want to help, meet me there with a big boat. If I need you, I'll use our call sign, 'I miss you.'"

July 23, 2013; Moscow, Russia, Sheremetyevo Airport Hotel

Nikoly Orlov walked into the hotel room of Edward Snowden, shaking hands with the lawyer he'd traveled with.

"You the lawyer?"

"Yes."

"Mind if we speak alone?"

"Not if Ed doesn't."

* * * *

At a table, looking at the sunset out the window, Orlov looked Snowden square in the face. He looked thinner than his pictures in the western newspapers, Orlov thought.

"We just don't know what to do with you, young man," he finally said.

"Thank you for your candor," Snowden said, smiling tightly. "But I think I knew that already."

"I understand you brought a trove of information with you when you left Hawaii," Orlov said. "But you didn't leave any with China."

Snowden shrugged noncommittally.

Orlov narrowed his eyes.

"Edward, tell me why you stole these secrets – what motivates you?"

Snowden looked around, blinking.

"Information belongs to everyone equally. My government is watching what we are all writing and doing. The U.S. has even built hundreds of algorithms that could be used in influence ops."

Orlov raised his eyebrows.

"What do you want to do? We can't find a place for you to land. The U.S. has reissued you a U.S. passport that allows you to board a plane bound for the U.S. only. They have a trial planned for you. You cannot win."

"I don't – I just knew what we were doing was wrong and I had to tell the world."

Orlov leaned back, rubbing his chin.

"You didn't say what you wanted to do. There is a way

to teach the U.S. a lesson. Let me make you a job offer. I run a team you may be interested in joining, but you must bring something to the table."

Snowden closed his eyes. This was the moment.

September 1, 2013; Outside Moscow, Russia, Tutin's Dacha

Walking through the gardens behind the spacious home, Orlov walked with Tutin.

"Snowden decided," Orlov told the president.

"He joins our team next week. He gave up the drives he took from Hawaii. Here's the best part. The Americans have been perfecting algorithms to be used in influence operations, but have not deployed them yet."

Tutin smiled. "Oops."

His old friend smiled back. "Some are very similar to what we've come up with. Some others are genius. I almost want them to find us using them."

"So this is information you didn't already have."

"That's correct. His defection came at the perfect time. Americans and Europeans have been consumed about what to do with spies here and around Europe."

"Good."

"I'm expanding our troll farms again," Orlov said. "We have much more to do."

November 8, 2013; Moscow, Miss Universe Pageant Reception

Jules prowled around the event flirting, laughing and oozing sexiness.

She finally caught Woody's eye across the room. He started toward her.

She pretended to be surprised he noticed her.

"What's your name, beautiful?" He asked huskily,

standing too close.

"I'm Jules – oh, Mr. Woody, I never thought I'd get to meet you, how are you? Ready for tomorrow night?"

"Yeah, we'll be fine." He kept doing the abuser's dance of trying to get in her personal space. Jules danced too, trying stay at arm's length of him, although she needed for him to make a move on her.

Suddenly, Woody turned away, then back around – and stepped in close enough to scoot his hand up her skirt, between her thighs.

Jules grabbed his hand, twisting it powerfully, turning the much larger man around and pushing him through a door, ending with his back up against a wall, all the while controlling him by holding his thumb back too far.

"Ow, ow, ow," he whimpered, staying bent over to keep his thumb from breaking.

"You wanna touch something, Mr. Woody, touch yourself," she said, pushing his hand she was holding roughly into his crotch and then releasing it and stepping backwards.

"Hey, you didn't have to do that," he gasped, rubbing his hand.

"Yes, but it was fun for me. You should behave. Enjoy Moscow." She spun, and dashed away.

"Wait, wait. You run a security service, right?"

She stopped, suppressing a smile. She had him right where she wanted him. He needed to possess that which he could not have.

Clearly, he'd asked about her before his clumsy-ass approach.

Slowly she turned around, hands on her hips, weighing all the angles.

Very slowly Jules walked back toward him, so slow her feet seemed heavy.

"I don't trust that you really want security – I expect you will try that pussy grabbing business again."

"No, I really do want the security. My kids are here from time to time. I'm gonna build hotels here. Already got financing all lined up."

He was back in his braggy-swagger mode, rubbing his now-sore thumb.

She pulled her card out of her purse and held it out of his reach.

"If you want security, you want my company. The FBI trained me. If you just need to fuck somebody, I can refer you."

She waved the card as if to make a point. "Deal's for great security, no sex. If you somehow forget, we're done."

"Deal. But if you change your mind …"

"Security, no sex. Not changing my mind," she said rapidly, with her hardest no-nonsense face.

"Deal." He handed her a card. "Send me a contract here."

She took the card, backed up, nodded, and gave him a dazzling smile.

"I'll do that. You be good."

She turned and walked away, waving goodbye, while giving him a slight butt wiggle to remember.

She emailed him a contract the next day, in the event he was serious.

GETTING THE ROOKIE TO RUN

November 10, 2013; Near Moscow, President Tutin's Dacha

The cabal whose intention was to fuck democracy gathered to talk to their friend, Dale Woody. Just to show Woody how serious he was, Tutin himself hosted this gathering.

Over dinner, the group — which included all the Russians at Sochi earlier that year, plus Mantribe — thanked him for bringing the pageant to Moscow.

They proceeded to encourage and cajole him.

"Are you going to run for president?" Sopranov asked.

Woody shrugged.

"Every businessman is a statesman, you'd be a natural," said President Tutin.

"With your business success and notoriety, you will be the automatic front-runner," said one of the oligarchs.

"Nobody else will have such a beautiful wife," said another.

They all knew the book on him. Narcissist. The attention span of a gnat. Serial sexual abuser. Entirely about money.

Exactly the kind of guy they needed to succeed in American politics to help them push the U.S. out of Europe, and to the wings of the world stage.

* * * *

Jules was in a tree, about two miles away, powerful binoculars to her face.

A muscular male associate was with her, both were wearing black. Her associate was looking at a screen, earbud in his ear.

"Please tell me we are getting sound from this," she said.

"Sorry, chief. They must have a whiteout type deal running."

She closed her eyes in frustration, letting her head fall back. "Guess if it was easy, anybody could do it, huh?"

* * * *

President Tutin stood to lead a toast, signaling the others to remain seated.

"Let me tell you what our intentions are," Tutin lied. "We are upon a new day between our nations, on a cusp of peace that will generate so much economic activity, nobody can lose."

Tutin walked to Woody and shook his hand saying, "Forgive me for leaving early. My granddaughter's concert begins in a few minutes. Enjoy the brandy and dessert. I hope to see you again soon as U.S. President."

"Thank you. Me too," Woody replied.

Tutin and several others strode out, leaving just Sopranov, Splater, Mantribe and Woody in the room.

"Guess it's gonna be a good concert. I usually fall asleep at concerts," Woody smiled, shrugging.

"I want to pay you for job," Sopranov said to Woody abruptly.

"OK."

"For serious. I give you $50 million to run for Republican nomination until you win or lose."

Woody looked incredulous. Then he looked at Mantribe, "He serious?"

"I am," Sopranov assured him. "If you win Republican nomination, there's $50 million performance bonus."

"That fee is for you alone, Dale. They also cover the cost of the campaign."

Woody, ever the negotiator, put his hands together and turned to Sopranov.

"I want to build a hotel here in Moscow, but am having trouble getting it financed."

Sopranov stayed cool, knowing that was the kind of investment that would run into the billions. He didn't blink, even knowing Woody was notorious about not repaying loans.

"We will make papers – contract – before you leave, so you know financing is ready for you."

"AND …" Woody never stopped. "In the event I don't win the whole thing, I'll need a new gig, and an investor. Maybe a cable station, like Fox News."

"Excellent idea. I will either direct an investor to you for this, or I will invest myself. Believe me, we will help you in every way possible."

"That's true, Dale," Mantribe confided.

Sopranov cut his eyes at Mantribe.

"What do you want from me?" Woody asked.

"If you win, grant U.S. energy technology transfers, we want to start fracking. We want to be friends, build both economies. Back away from NATO – the Cold War is over. Then, do whatever the fuck you want," he smiled.

November 11, 2013; Moscow, Russia

Jules' contract was returned and a deposit for her faux-company's services was already in the bank. From what she knew of Woody, that was unusual.

Woody called her. "So, now you work for me. Can you pick me up, work security for us tonight?"

"Sure. Remember, no sex – and that I can literally kill you with my little finger."

"Six o'clock."

* * * *

When she arrived to fetch the man-child sexual abuser, she sent the driver to his room to get him.

"I thought you'd be coming to my room," said Woody, as he settled into the backseat by Jules.

"Oh, I was busy looking for threats," she smiled absently.

"Well …" he reached for her thigh.

She pulled out an oversized pistol she never used. But knowing Woody's respect for all things big, she figured it wouldn't hurt.

She immediately began to unload and reload the gun loudly.

Woody withdrew his hand and became enthralled with the street scenes they were passing.

* * * *

The destination was a party, which included Splater, Mantribe, Nikolay Orlov, and six Russian female spies posing as hookers.

The party quickly devolved into a big orgy, with lots of bad boy behavior.

November 14, 2013; Moscow flat of Jules Archer

Jules rose early to see if there was anything useful on the tapes, but it was entirely old men having sex with younger women.

At one point, Mantribe and Orlov joked about, "a different sort of insurrection," as a sexual innuendo.

Jules' ears perked up at "insurrection," but other than using that word, the men were altogether unhelpful with what they were otherwise up to.

Jules frowned, frustrated at her inability to connect these people and their intentions to how Russia intended to screw her country.

Late February, 2014

Days after concluding the most expensive Olympics in history, one that showcased the best of Russia, Moscow invaded Ukraine. A former Soviet Republic, the nation was interested in NATO membership to protect them from an increasingly aggressive Russia.

Too late, obviously.

It was Mantribe's Tumultus, the massive influence campaign in Europe and the United States, that made the Ukrainian invasion seem less sinful than it was.

NATO's calculation was that protecting Ukraine militarily would put the European continent into a third world war, even as the western democracies' militaries were straining under the decade-plus commitments in Afghanistan and Iraq … and the growing concern around ISIS, now in Syria, Iraq and Libya.

Rather than go at it militarily, the least bad option for the U.S. and western democracies was to cry foul, try to shame Russia on the world stage, and impose increasingly painful economic sanctions on Russia.

March 6, 2014; Moscow, Russia, Kremlin, Presidential office

"He did what?" Tutin yelled.

The assistant cleared his throat to repeat it. "Barack Obama just ordered new U.S. sanctions: a travel ban, and he's freezing U.S. assets against certain Russians, specifically you, and a couple of generals who invested in U.S. real estate."

"FUCK!" He strode to the window to stare out. "What of fracking technology transfers?"

"He didn't include that, but expect that is coming."

Tutin breathed in deeply and shook his head.

"The good news is our invasion force is already there."

May 18, 2014; Prague, Czech Republic

Just outside Prague in a luxurious, fully-staffed lake house, Nikolay Orlov greeted Kent Mantribe in the driveway.

* * * *

"Tell me of our friend," Orlov said to Mantribe, as the men watched the sun set from a rooftop balcony.

* * * *

Pierre and a colleague watched from high in a tree far away, binoculars to their faces.

"Do we have a mic on the rooftop?" he asked.

"No, every room in the fucking house, just not outside," the other Frenchman said.

Pierre breathed out loudly. "Ahhhhhh."

* * * *

"Dale's good, sends his best," Mantribe said. "I have an idea for you to consider. The cyber-influencing operation is working well. Let's focus our aim at a specific target: Congress."

"Won't that risk exposing it?"

"No. We can actually run a micro-campaign, see how our new social media tactics work on key staffers for Members of Congress. At the very least, that applies maximum pressure right now, exactly where you want it."

* * * *

In a meeting room, Mantribe and Orlov sat at opposite ends of a grand table. The 20 seats between them were filled with young geeks, notebooks open.

Orlov began by gesturing to Mantribe. "Kent has helped us with this work before."

"Lobbying is no more than an influencing operation, a one-to-one operation," Mantribe began. "But the exciting thing about what we are doing is directing that influence at the voting population. Which is what campaigns do."

Geeks around the table were taking notes – no electronic tablets were allowed in the meeting.

"You will be leading our permanent campaign and we will stay in regular contact through Nikolay."

"Our first order of business will be the Congress experiment, then we turn our attention to the 2016 elections," Orlov said.

* * * *

In the summer of 2014, the despair of Sochi's Olympic Village creaked with silence and stillness. A desolation of fading vodka ads and Olympic Rings.

The place that just months ago housed the world's greatest athletes competing in the winter Olympics, saw its first real activity since tourists abandoned it altogether after the Ukrainian invasion.

It was insular, out of the way, lots of room, and nobody ever went there.

The perfect place for a troll farm.

Orlov's team repurposed the giant media center for a central workplace.

Team members arrived in such overwhelming numbers that Orlov moved a luxury cruise liner offshore to house even more trolls and offered another secure workplace.

September 11, 2014; Moscow, Russia, Kremlin, Tutin's Office

Tutin read the news story on a tablet, headlined: *"Obama: U.S. Imposes Russian Sanctions; Punishment for Ukraine invasion."*

The story, *"The U.S. and E.U. imposed tougher sanctions on Russia's financial, energy and defense sectors, putting over $8 trillion in Russian oil reserves just out of Russia's reach."*

Obama said, "Russian aggression is a greater threat to U.S. democracy than terrorism."

ASSASSINS TAKE AIM

Tutin was furious. He slammed his fist on the desk.

"Shit! Who else has the technology?"

"China has inferior technology – that's why we needed it from United States," said his staffer.

He hated telling the president bad news; but he might as well rip the Band-Aid all the way off.

The staffer cleared his throat.

"The individual financial sanctions this time includes Sopranov's bank and the banks of the other oligarchs," he said quietly.

Tutin fumed, but let it go, remembering what he let loose inside the U.S. – and international banking systems.

October 24, 2014; Washington, D.C., FBI Headquarters

"Pierre's success in capturing sound inside the May weekend in Prague gave us a leg up in following the manipulation techniques Moscow is perfecting," Zack told Director Commings.

"Now we – and several spy agencies – are watching Moscow's intelligence operations in the U.S.," Zack continued. "Here's me burying the lead. As we speak, Russian agents are applying their new social media tactics on key aides to members of Congress."

"NO!" said Director Commings.

Zack had his full attention before, but the giant FBI Director could no longer sit. He stretched out his 6'4" frame and came around the desk to sit by Zack.

"Orlov's troll farms broadcast material on social media to see how targets respond to their calls for action on whatever," Zack continued.

"So the Russians are using their manipulation campaign on Hill staffers?" Director Commings asked, rubbing his face. "All to see who is susceptible and who would be more favorable to what they want to do?"

"Yes, sir," Zack said slowly. "Since we now know the goal is to somehow influence the 2016 election, we think this is … an experiment of sorts. Mantribe described it like that, almost like training for the final act."

Zack paused.

"So, do we tell Congress? We lose a lot in the investigation if we do. Congress isn't so much a target as a practice session. We may get more out of it by going quiet, continuing to observe. Maybe that'll help us see what they are doing in the 2016 cycle."

The director stared at the ceiling.

"This is gonna be tricky," he said slowly. "No, we don't tell Congress what we know today, it's too fragmented. Maybe I'll drop it in as 'interesting' next time I'm with the group of eight," referring to the bipartisan leadership of Congress, "Ask they ratchet up IT security."

March 29, 2015; Moscow, Russia, Café off Red Square

Jules sat at a corner table.

Pierre came in fast from the kitchen, not the front entrance.

She saw him and raised her eyebrows.

"Come with me, love," he said quietly, but urgently, pulling her by the arm

"I'm supposed to meet-"

"Shhhh."

They reached the kitchen and scurried through the distracted workers and ran to his car.

They tore out, turning onto the street. They passed the Russian Jules was to meet.

"That's my meeting," she pointed, unseen by the Russian.

"He's an assassin," Pierre said. "Here," he pushed a phone and earbuds toward her.

He watched her listen. She rolled her eyes. "Shit."

"Your cover's blown, love. Where to?"

Prague, Czech Republic; CIA Safe House

Zack sat with Steve Champion watching Mantribe's most recent meeting with Nikoly Orlov.

"When did you update the dossier last?" Zack asked.

"Last night actually." Champion kept a detailed dossier – a list really – of the sins this team and their western counterparts around the world had discovered in the years-long investigation into Russia's intention to derail NATO and the U.S.

"Told the Director you have that. He was a little surprised the western spies worked together so closely in Moscow."

"Ever since the Cold War, mate."

"Hang together or hang separately?"

"Exactly – that's what your Benjamin Franklin argued in the Continental Congress."

Smiling and nodding 'yes', Zack looked at his phone.

"From Pierre…" he frowned, reading the message: "Jules' ID compromised. She's gone to safe house. Said she missed you."

Zack swallowed hard and stood up fast.

"Shit. I need a flight to Baku."

Champion grabbed his phone. "I'll take care of that."

Zack quickly punched his phone, calling the FBI Agent in Charge in Baku, Azerbaijan, a young man he'd recommended for the post last year.

"Jose, I'm gonna be in your neck of the woods by morning. How's the sturgeon fishing? You're always bragging about it. I'm free until evening."

"Great, I'll get us a boat," said the voice on the phone. They hung up.

"Need me with you?" Champion asked.

Zack hesitated. "No, you stay here," he waved his finger at the screen showing Mantribe and Orlov. "Keep an eye on them. I got agents in Baku."

March 30, 2015; Shchelkovo, Russia, Spy Training Academy

Two hooded figures on foot wearing night vision gear carefully approached the outer fence.

The larger figure pulled a tarp off a hole outside the fence.

"Ready to go gopher, chief?" asked the bulky young man.

Jules smiled and lowered herself into the hole headfirst, coming up on the opposite side of the fence, filthy.

The two moved silently in darkness toward the facility.

* * * *

A guard stood outside, smoking.

From one side, Jules cooed softly in Russian, "Who called for the hooker?"

When the guard looked her way, Jules' colleague grabbed him from the other side, twisting his neck to a sickening pop.

Jules took the guard's radio and keys.

* * * *

In the dark building, Jules unlocked a door.

* * * *

Inside the room, flashlights in their mouths, they looked around. Jules sat down at a computer. She put a large volume jump drive in, and began a download.

* * * *

"Done," Jules said, placing the fourth drive in a plastic bag.

"Hey, here's a couple more drives," her comrade said, opening drawers. He dropped them in a plastic bag.

She put the whiskey bottle shaped drives – the four she'd just copied, plus the two just discovered – underneath her body armor.

They turned off the flashlights, and pulled night vision gear over their eyes.

* * * *

Voices behind them spurred them to go faster. The voices got louder and footsteps headed after them.

They ran down a stairwell. Bullets fired behind them.

In a hallway, they ran toward a door, but two guards blocked their way. They turned around, went down more stairs, and found themselves in a steam pipe room.

Jules pointed and bullets flew.

Jules and the man ran toward the door, dodging bullets.

"Shit!" he gasped, blood spurting out of his mouth.

Jules stopped as he fell onto his back.

"GO! Get it out. GO!"

She blanched, but put his gun in his hand, pointing it where they came from, and ran fast, not looking back.

As she opened the door leading out, she heard an intense exchange of gunfire behind her.

She ran low across the ground toward the fence, bullets whizzing past her.

She dove into the hole, staying on the ground on the other side of the fence, crawling fast to the nearby tree line.

* * * *

Jules mounted a motorcycle, taking off in the dark Russian night, sounds of yelling and dogs barking fading, as she put distance between them.

* * * *

Jules pulled over under some trees to bandage her upper arm, which was oozing blood from a bullet wound.

She sped off again.

* * * *

At a farm, she went to a barn, and opened the big doors. Jules used the motorcycle to pull out a small plane. The wings were folded up.

She began readying the plane, wincing when she used her arm.

* * * *

The plane took off from a field.

* * * *

Already in the north Caspian area by mid-morning, Zack and his team had been tracking the plane as it flew closer to their boat.

Zack and three others were on the bridge; two of the three wore FBI windbreakers, the other was a crusty sea captain.

One agent looked at the screen.

"She's descending – about five minutes out," said the first agent.

"What's that?" said the second agent, pointing at a blip on the edge of the screen.

"Holy shit. I think that's a MiG. Fuck. He's shooting!" said the first agent.

"No-" Zack froze.

"Zack, I think he's got her," said the captain.

"NO! Trajectory's off; too low, he missed," said the second agent.

Zack breathed out in relief.

"Shooting again. Damnit!" said the captain.

* * * *

Nearing the edge of the Caspian, Jules saw the MIG's missile headed straight for her this time. It hit the tail, knocking it off.

The plane spun around, pinning Jules against the side. The plane began a rapid descent, just over the water.

* * * *

The captain kicked the boat into high gear, steering it toward the falling plane.

* * * *

Since this was her long-hidden escape, this old-looking plane had a modern naval ejection seat, minus the ink to show her location in the water.

She heroically pushed away from the side of the plane to reach the trigger behind her head. Suddenly, the seat back exploded through the glass top, and that activated her parachute and a body flotation device a few seconds later.

* * * *

"Everybody keep an eye on the plane," Zack said nervously. "She has an ejection seat. There, see it? Oh God," he kept repeating, his hands fidgeting. "Oh God."

"Got her," said the captain. "Eighteen degrees west, all speed."

* * * *

In the north Caspian Sea, just off the Azerbaijan coast, Jules hit the cold water hard, but it didn't kill her.

She thought she was swimming, but it was the inflated vest pulling her to the surface. She broke the surface and saw land in the distance.

She tried hard to move, teeth chattering as shock set into her body.

She heard the boat engine and her heart sank. Shit. She

was discovered.

"No," her blue lips moved. The sound was getting closer. A light shined in her face. She waited for the bullet.

A zodiac with two men, in all black, reached for her.

She didn't want to be taken alive, but she couldn't feel her arms and legs anymore. Her brain went numb.

* * * *

Jules woke up.

She was sure she was dreaming, then she remembered the race out of Russia.

She drew in her breath sharply and raised her head.

"Steady, now."

She smiled gratefully at Zack, sitting at a table nearby tapping on a laptop.

"Oh, man, am I glad to see you," she breathed with relief.

He kissed her on the forehead and moved her hair off her face; there were lots of cuts and bruises scattered around her pretty face. A face that looked fragile now.

"Babe, you got no idea how glad I am to see you," he said gently.

Suddenly, she remembered the drives she stole, absently touching her side.

"I was wearing … a vest," she gasped.

"Yep. A vest with a shitload of large volume drives in plastic underneath it. Already on the way back home." Looking at his watch, he added, "May be there by now."

She breathed out in relief, for the first time in years, it seemed.

"As soon as you can travel, I'm taking you away. Go ahead, fight with me about it. President himself has ordered you away from Moscow station."

He took a deep breath, stroking her head and holding her hand. "You in pain?"

"Sore, I think."

"Doc said any longer in the water, your lungs would have stopped. Got a couple of bruised ribs, a dislocated shoulder, pneumonia and a concussion. Plus cuts and bruises – and a gunshot wound, in the dislocated arm."

He patted her hand. "You are all put back together."

"Why do you look so worried?

"You can't travel yet and the Russians are looking for you," Zack said gently.

* * * *

Zack helped Jules sit at table near the bed.

Jules looked thoughtful. "If they are looking for me and we can't run, let 'em think I'm dead. That's an effective cover."

Zack, arms crossed, frowned.

April 5, 2015; Baku, Azerbaijan, United States Embassy

The U.S. Ambassador to Azerbaijan escorted Jules' father into the embassy morgue, "You ready, Sheriff Archer?"

The sheriff nodded.

"I'm so sorry to meet you like this," said Zack softly, shaking his hand. Zack unzipped the body bag until Jules' face was visible.

Sheriff Archer wept. "That's her. That's my baby girl."

"Madam Ambassador, I'll walk the Sheriff back to your office."

"My deepest sympathies to your family, sir; Agent

Archer was an extraordinary spy."

Archer had turned to the Ambassador when she offered condolences, and then watched her leave.

When the door closed, Jules said softly, "Daddy, I'm not dead."

Sheriff Archer spun back toward Jules, but backed up at the same time. In true Sheriff fashion, he reached for a gun at his side, although he didn't have one on.

"What the fuck!"

"Sheriff Archer," Zack gestured to chairs by the slab Jules was laying on.

"Let's sit. Sorry to jerk you around like that, but we need the Ambassador to believe she died. She's gonna convey this officially now, so the Russians will stop looking for Jules."

Sheriff Archer sat in the chair beside Jules, holding her hand and stroking her hair, unable to take his eyes off of her now, examining her hands, finding the tiny freckle on her upper lip, the birthmark on the side of her neck.

"You know Jules was never vilified by the FBI," Zack said gently. "That set up her cover for the CIA in Moscow. She was promoted to top spy after catching her chief when he was assassinated beside her."

Sheriff Archer's mouth fell open.

"She left Russia after they sniffed her out, too, but for good measure she stole a trove of information about a massive campaign they are running against us. She got shot stealing it, and then got shot out of the sky as she got to the Caspian."

"Oh, jeez. Jules, you're killing me, baby girl," Sheriff Archer said, putting his head on her arm.

She turned painfully onto her side to cradle his head, a tear slipping down her face.

"We plucked her out of the sea," Zack finished up.

"She's got pneumonia and a concussion so we can't leave and the Russians are beating the bushes for her."

"So this time, Daddy, my cover will be that I'm dead, give them a little head fake."

"But we need you to take what will appear to be her body home in a flag draped coffin and have a private burial. You can finally tell her brothers that she was a hero spy."

"In a few months, will you ask Max to take you to London, so we can see each other and have a visit?" she asked, suddenly missing her family

Hand on her face, smiling, he said, "You bet baby."

He paused, suddenly skeptical.

"We let you name the dog when you were five. What-"

"Lassie," she giggled. So like her dad, to test her.

"So that law enforcement thing's genetic," Zack deadpanned.

April 6, 2015; Azerbaijan, Baku International Airport

Outside a private hanger — so the Russians following them could see them loading a casket — Sheriff Archer and Zack saluted the casket as it was laid on the baggage conveyor by the honor guard.

After the casket was inside, Sheriff Archer bent over, hands on his knees. Zack gently pulled him back up. The men put their hands on each other's shoulders, heads together as the engine made listening to them impossible.

As they parted, they wiped tears and shook hands. The Sheriff boarded. Zack ran to the SUV, and took off.

* * * *

Zack drove northwest from Baku, passing a sign for

Shamakhi, Azerbaijan.

He pulled into a garage, the door closing behind him, and he activated the shield from eavesdropping devices.

He opened the back of the SUV and unzipped the fabric hiding the place under the back seat where Jules was safely hidden away.

Jules winked, "We ever go that long without talking?"

He shook his head, smiling.

* * * *

They pulled out in another vehicle, Jules in a makeshift bed in the back seat – an IV drip still going.

April 13, 2015; New York City, NY, Splater's Penthouse

Splater opened the door, greeting Mantribe, "Kent, I'm so glad to see you." The old friends embraced.

"Meet General Marc Glenn; Marc, Alex Splater."

"My honor, General," Splater said. "I've followed your career at the Defense Intelligence Agency."

General Glenn led the Agency from 2012-14, where he cultivated Russia as an ally against Islamist militants, even spending time with Russian military intelligence.

When General Glenn angrily and publicly insisted that Russia should be an ally even after invading Ukraine and seizing Crimea, President Obama fired the mouthy general.

"I hear you are consulting now, General; I would love to do business with you," Splater said.

"I'm trying to get him into politics," Kent grinned.

Glenn smiled his famous aw-shucks grin, "Hey, no fighting over me, boys."

Before the year was over, General Glenn would earn

hundreds of thousands of dollars from companies linked to the Russian mob and Russia's intelligence services.

April 15, 2015; Gabala, Azerbaijan CIA Safe House

On the overlook outdoor porch, Zack and Jules – whose long, dark locks were now shoulder-length and dyed blonde – shared an outdoor tea at sunset.

"It's really beautiful here," she said, running the back of her hand intimately along the back of his. "But I'm much stronger. How long do we stay here?"

He half-smiled and turned toward her.

"You are much better, but you're still pretty weak, babe. Maybe we stay till you beat me in a race."

"So, 24 hours?" she joked.

He rolled his eyes. "Champ's setting up a flat for you in London, we're finalizing your new ID. Task Force has a place in Prague, watching Mantribe visit there with the Russian geeks and Orlov. The French have it up."

"Any word from Pierre?"

"Still in Moscow, no word otherwise."

"I owe him."

"Me too. You stayed too long, babe."

"Was it worth it?"

"Better believe it."

BREAKING THE BANK

April 18, 2015

"John Doe" transmitted documents from a Central American law firm – suspected of laundering money for rich Russians – to a German news organization.

The release comprised what would be called the "Panama Papers" – emails, letters, photographs and client data – which ultimately added up to 11.5 million individual files, equivalent to 2.6 terabytes of data.

Summer, 2015; Sochi, Russia, Troll Farm

Orlov sat with several geeks around a table on a deck with faded Olympic rings prominent and a fabulous view of the Black Sea with the splash of its angry waves.

"We figured out a way to hack into primary elections in Florida – hack into voter rolls, change party ID," began one of the geeks. "Republicans in south Florida coming to vote for Marco Rubio – if he's even still in it – will discover they are not registered as a Republican."

"We can replicate it with other target states, but Dash says Woody can win Florida if we push Rubio down. He could be a late threat, so we do this to Florida first."

Another geek began excitedly, "We are experimenting with malware to use in our targets in November. We will be able to move a small percentage of votes from one candidate to the other in voting machines."

"I know you can," Sopranov winked. "We have spies working in election offices around those target states."

June 16, 2015; London, England

Jules, her hair much shorter now and more white than blonde, ran along a London street at daybreak.

Passing a newsstand, the headline of a London paper read: *"Woody Makes it Official, Will Seek Republican Nomination in U.S."*

* * * *

Barefoot in her flat, sitting at her laptop, Jules was interrupted by a knock.

A smile spread over her face and she ran to the door.

"Yes?" she checked.

"Police, open the door," her father's voice replied playfully.

Sheriff Archer and Jules' brother, Max, rushed in, grabbing her in a long, long hug.

Steve Champion walked in behind them rolling luggage.

When they finally acknowledged him, Champion said, "Don't leave the presents in the hall."

"You brought me presents?" she asked excitedly.

"Tiny, Butch," Sheriff Archer called out, as a German Shepherd and Great Dane bounded into the room.

Jules squealed in delight, getting down on the floor with the gigantic dogs.

"Figured you could use a little non-human back-watching, baby girl," said her father, smiling broadly.

"Remember Daddy's buddy that raises military dogs?" Max asked.

"These guys came from there?"

"Yep. Great Dane is Tiny. Butch is the Shepherd," the Sheriff said.

She got up to hug her father again, after which, Max grabbed her in another hug.

"OK, I'm out of here, cheerio," Champion said.

"Champ, thanks, really," Jules said, holding her hand out to Champion, her other arm still around her brother.

"I'll come back to take us to dinner tonight."

"How about we cook?" Sheriff Archer suggested.

"Sure. I'll send someone take you to get what you need," Champion looked serious. "Do not go out – and keep Jules in. We'll have a long talk tonight."

* * * *

That evening – with Butch sprawled in front of the door and Tiny near Jules' heels – Max finished setting the table as Butch jumped up, sniffed and let out a low growl.

Champion knocked on the door. "It's me."

"It's OK, Butch," Jules called out.

Max let him in, taking the bottle he offered.

"Smells great. American fare, I presume," Champion said, kissing Jules on the cheek and shaking hands with the Sheriff and Max.

"Hope you like ribs," Jules smiled.

* * * *

"Champ, is Jules a prisoner here?" asked Max casually, chewing on a rib.

Smiling, he said, "Hiding. She's dead, remember?"

"She's a coward, hiding here when Russia's moving on us like a bitch," Jules said softly, looking down.

Champion looked at her patiently.

"Coward my ass," Champion said. "She's got more balls than all of us. They found me in Russia after two years. Took the bastards four years to discover Jules."

He reached over and put his hand on her shoulder.

"She didn't just run when her cover got blown," Champion continued. "She hid outside Moscow for a couple of days to steal from their spy academy, got away with a ton of shit, including stuff Snowden gave them."

The Sheriff and Max listened mid-bite, mouths open.

"She flew out in a little plane and a Russian MiG blew her out of the sky. Zack fished her out of the Caspian, hid her till you got there, sir," he nodded to the Sheriff.

Silence.

"Shit, baby girl," said Max looking like a fascinated 12-year-old. "You're Jules Bond! What'd you steal?"

She shot him the I'm-not-going-to-tell-you-look a little sister gives her big brother.

"Intelligence."

"Anything you *can* tell us?" her father asked, sitting forward. "We're here. We already know you ain't dead."

"Right," she said slowly. "I still belong to the CIA. I'm working with Zack and Champ on …."

She looked at Champion, imploring him.

"Here, let me keep you from breaking the law. Daddy'd hate that," Champion smiled. "The Russians are trying to steal your 2016 presidential election. We found a gigantic influence operation – but there are other pieces we don't have our hands around."

"That'd never happen," declared Sheriff Archer.

"Hell, an influence campaign here – from Russia with love – to get us to leave the European Union may well make it to the ballot," Champion said in frustration.

* * * *

Champion stood at the door, shaking hands and kissing Jules goodbye on the cheek.

"We'll get out of London this weekend, give you a change of scenery," he said. "I have a country house with lots of rooms, space, horses, all that."

He patted the dogs. "Give these guys some running room."

September 18, 2015; Washington, D.C., FBI Headquarters

The sign on the door read, SNOWDEN TASK FORCE.

"They hacked the DNC?" Director Commings asked his team incredulously.

"Yeah, basically stripped them dry," Zack said evenly. "If we tip them off, we give up to the Russians that we're watching."

"Don't you think they know that now? Two of the drives Jules Archer stole before she died were from Snowden," the Director reminded him. "They have to assume we have them back, or know of their theft."

The Director knew exactly where Jules was, but followed the story precisely unless he and Zack were alone.

"Too close to the presidential race," said one of the team members sitting on a desk.

"Which is a fucking mess," Zack added.

"Just as the Russians wanted," said a second team member stretching against a wall.

"There's also a report of Russian agents working in IT there, and at the RNC," said the first agent.

"What if our cyber office cold-calls the DNC, tells

them at least one computer's been hacked by an espionage team linked to Russia," Zack offered. "We can see where that goes."

* * * *

The agent who called was transferred to an IT contractor at the DNC help desk, who checked the DNC's server logs. Assuming it was a weird scam, the contractor didn't reply to the FBI agent's follow-up call.

November 1, 2015; Near Newport, England

Jules ran to Zack like an old lover – or 'friend with benefits.'

Champion, Sheriff Archer and Max uncomfortably watched from the porch as the two shared a long kiss while the dogs danced around.

"Oh, I've missed you," Zack whispered in her ear.

"Missed you more."

As the dogs sniffed him, Zack grabbed her hand and waved at the others, walked over and shared hugs and handshakes.

* * * *

In the bedroom the next morning, Jules and Zack laid together quietly.

"Feel like talking about the investigation?" she whispered.

Putting the back of his forearm on his head, Zack exhaled and said, "Hard to know where to start."

A sound outside caused Jules to sit up and check the vehicle driving up.

She drew in her breath excitedly.

"It's Pierre."

She jumped out of bed, naked.

"Put on clothes, babe."

* * * *

Sitting on a rooftop deck, their conversation shielded from listening devices, the band was finally back together.

Now joined by Max and Sheriff Archer, Champion, Jules, Zack and Pierre laughed and scared the shit out of her family by rehashing Jules' narrow escape from Russia.

Zack looked at the Sheriff and Max.

"I'm reading you two in on this investigation, you're already aware of some of it, and we need to talk about it now. You repeat anything to anybody and I'll kill you myself."

"That's not true," Pierre snarked. "He'd make somebody else do it."

"Live Russian trolls number about 75,000 now," said Zack, giving Pierre the side eye.

"The influence operation is the part we can see the best, the part that ain't illegal, the part Americans could ignore if we only had the ability to."

He frowned and shook his head.

"More and more, I'm worried we have missed something," Zack continued. "The influence campaign is not all they are doing. Jules, one of the drives you stole had a video of spy cadets learning to vote at a machine — but no context. Could be to teach culture."

"Could be to steal your election," Pierre said to Zack, his head nodding.

"Hacking, you mean," Champion said.

"Right," Pierre said.

Jules closed her eyes. She left so much undone in Russia, and was now too far out of place to figure anything out. Suddenly, she was back in Russia, next to her chief – the next instant she was covered in blood.

Her eyes opened, her breathing quickened.

"Just before my chief died, he was telling me about a massive influx of spies into the spy academy. That's one of the reasons I went there on the way out."

She opened her mouth, then seemed lost in thought.

"I don't know … why this didn't occur to me before," she said slowly, quietly. "Is moving a buttload of cadets to your spy academy the intelligence equivalent of massing on somebody's border?"

"What are you thinking, Jules?" Zack said. "They are using spies to vote?"

"That's crazy," her father said quietly.

"Maybe," she said slowly, still turning matters over in her head. "Maybe just putting feet on the ground to support whatever hacking they are planning."

The group had narrowed eyes and cocked heads as they wrapped their heads around that possibility.

* * * *

"If Russia sent a shitload of spies to Europe or the U.S. – that'd strain their logistics presumably, right?" Max asked as Sheriff Archer served up slices of cake.

"What are you getting at?" Jules asked him.

"Moving people, supporting them – especially covertly – costs money. How are they paying for it?"

"That is expensive, and you are right. We should be able to follow the money," Champion said. "We are very good at that."

"But the trail always stops in Switzerland or the

Caymans," Zach said.

"You know I'm working in our London branch now." Max paused, seeming to weigh something ... trying to make a decision. He ran his hand through his hair, stared away, and slowly looked at the people around the table.

Suddenly fascinated by his hands, he said, "I've seen some interesting transactions while I've been there."

As one, Champion, Jules, Zack and Pierre all leaned forward ever so slightly, their eyes blinking and moving, faces showing micro tics as they ran rapidly though what they knew, could find out, and didn't know ... and measuring how smart it was to include a non-club member in any aspect of this.

Clearing his throat carefully, Champion said pleasantly, "What department are you in, Max?"

"Compliance," he said, swallowing.

Eyes even wider in surprise, the task force members all begin to fidget – weighing what they were about to do.

Taking a breath, Champion plunged in. "You do!"

Hands up, knowing what was coming, Jules said firmly, "No. Wait."

Sheriff Archer, seeing her expression and having an inkling what was coming, joined in.

"Why are you three," he pointed at Champion, Zack and Pierre, "Looking at Max like a hungry man looks at food?"

"I get it, Sheriff – Jules. Let me ... just ..." Zack held up his hands reassuringly to Jules, his eyes on Max.

"Do you know what Russian mob money looks like-"

Max looked insulted. "Of course. It's the stuff you know is wrong, but the paperwork is all in order and you ain't supposed to question shit about it."

"Max," Jules finally jumped in. "No." She looked sat her father in exasperation. "Daddy...."

She refocused her attention. Holding her hand up to her team, signaling this was her ball to carry, she began gently.

"Max, this is not just about banking. We are spying – on the Russians. Who would much rather kill you than let you go. We train for this stuff for years."

"You wouldn't be ready son," Sheriff Archer said to the one child *not* enamored by law enforcement.

That surprised his youngest son, and somehow stung a little, like all that talk how he was a black sheep because he succeeded in a different venue from law enforcement.

His breath escaped, but he quickly recovered.

Leaning back, hands behind his head, Max said arrogantly, "Well, it seems to me that you don't so much need somebody to bust in doors. You need a banker."

"We have bankers," Zack said evenly.

"Do you have one on the inside?" Max snapped back. He stood up.

"Look, I get y'all are worried," he said softly in his tilting Georgia accent that made ladies on Wall Street swoon just a little bit. "I was the math geek that didn't get a job carrying a gun. But who's to say I didn't get the law enforcement gene?"

He eyed his father and little sister.

"Come on, don't be mad. Hey, I'm a patriot, too. What if the Russians are really trying to steal an election? Isn't this all hands on deck?"

His question hung for a few seconds until Pierre leaned towards the Sheriff, his hand on the older man's arm, saying, "He just might have that gene."

* * * *

They spent the next hours questioning him.

"Your bank have offices in the Caymans and Switzerland?"

"Yes, both. We all play there. Same reason Willie Sutton robbed banks. That's where the money is."

"What exactly do you have access to?"

Smiling, Max pulled out the very full leather briefcase the family gave him when he got the Wall Street job.

* * * *

Members of the team poured over banking records in stacks around the table, smiles all over everybody's face.

"We were exactly right," Zack said quietly.

"But we cannot use stolen work products," Jules said just as quietly. She locked her eyes on her brother.

"Max, what exactly do you think is going to happen?"

"Well, I'm definitely leaving my job."

"Your million dollar a year job?"

"Yes," he answered his sister. "Zack, does this buy me a place on your team?"

Zack opened his mouth to answer immediately, but stopped and looked first at Jules and Sheriff Archer. He couldn't read either face.

Looking back at Max, he said, "Yes it does."

* * * *

Early the next morning, the whole group was back up, pouring over Max's document dump.

Max, standing and leaning over behind Zack, pointed at the document Zack held.

"Shiiiit!" Zack smiled, eyes wide, turning to see Max smiling back.

"What?" the others said almost together.

"Last year, there was a leak from a law firm that sets up offshore companies for mostly rich Russians," Max said, walking around, rubbing his hands on his jeans.

"Panama Papers," said Pierre.

"So big that the German writer who got the documents called in the International Consortium of Investigative Journalists to help unravel everything. My bank is not directly implicated – but we do have an association with a bank that was."

"Reporters were asking questions, and – me being in compliance – when the questions came, the lawyers come to us for the ass-covering paperwork."

Hands on his hips now, Max looked satisfied.

"They even let me see documents from the leak when they wanted a response from us. Then I knew what to look for in our own files. This is what I found. Probably not what the Consortium has, or their questions of us would have been much different."

Sheriff Archer, head on his hands, asked, "Max, does your bank have an inkling what you are doing?"

"Nope, security is so bad there's still a paper file room in the branch here," Max said, looking at Champion and gesturing at the documents spread out on the table.

"These pages are missing from there. No personal possessions remain in the office. Soon, I'll send a note to my boss telling him I am eloping and honeymooning. Eventually, my new wife'll want to live someplace else and I take a leave of absence."

Max pulled up a chair beside his father.

"Daddy, I've made great money and like all good bankers, I've got a stash in the Caymans. When, or if, my bank discovers me, I'll no longer be an employee. Also, Pierre is right. I got that law enforcement gene."

Jules got up and hugged him from behind. "I believe

you did!"

"Plus, the Russians tried to kill my little sister to hide all this bullshit. I know it's dangerous. But it's my country, too. I'm in."

December 10, 2015; Miami, Florida

Over 200 Russian spies – who'd been in the U.S. for over two years now posing as Americans – gathered on a party boat for what was billed as a Christmas party for a business.

In reality, it was one last briefing for the Russian insurrection's team leaders.

* * * *

"As they say here, this is the 'nitty gritty' of politics," said the woman whose Russian accent was gone by the time she was 25 and a Russian spy in the U.S. She was the Kremlin's point person for the "boots" component of the 2016 election.

"This is a package for you to pass to your teams."

The efficient calendar attached to the front outlined how they would maximize voting methods in order for each boot to cast 25 votes in each target state.

PRIMARY CALENDAR
Feb. 8, Florida, apply for a mail-in ballot
Feb. 15, Michigan, apply for 23 ballots
Feb. 22, Michigan, mark, mail 23 ballots (Banders)
Feb. 29, Florida early voting begins
March 8, Michigan Election Day (Banders)
March 15, Florida Election Day
March 21, Wisconsin early voting begins

March 28, Pennsylvania, apply for 23 ballots
April 5, Wisconsin Election Day
April 6, Pennsylvania, mark, mail 23 ballots
April 26, Pennsylvania Election Day

GENERAL ELECTION CALENDAR

Sep. 19, Wisconsin early voting – 25 ballots ASAP
Oct. 14, Pennsylvania, apply for 23 mail-in ballots
Oct. 17, Michigan, apply for 25 mail-in ballots
Oct. 26, Florida early voting – 25 ballots by Oct 28
Oct. 29, Pennsylvania, mark, mail 23 ballots
Oct. 31, Michigan, mark, mail 25 ballots
Nov. 6, Pennsylvania, Election Day

"Florida is up first," said the spy briefer. "Make sure each boot casts a mail-in ballot to get used to that. We will depend on this method even more in the fall when the voting calendar is more abbreviated."

"Michigan's primary is March 8, and has no early voting. Michigan is the one place we vote in the Democratic primary, not the Republican, to slow down Clanton. Vote for Banders there."

"Remember, each character for each boot only votes one time in the primary and one time in November," she said. "Otherwise, we could be discovered."

January 18, 2016; Geneva, Switzerland

Pierre pulled into a parking place outside a grandiose, old Swiss bank. He tapped a whiteout app.

"Remember, I loiter in the front offices to make sure nobody tries to trap us. Max, follow the plan, get the data, and get out. Jules is only with you to cover your ass and figure the way out if anything gets dangerous."

"Anything goes south, we exit out the back," Jules said evenly.

"I know you're repeating it for my own good," Max smiled, clearly relaxed. "Thank you and I'd remembered. This is my playground. I know what I'm doing in a bank."

Pierre and Jules nodded. Jules swallowed hard; she'd have felt better if Max were a little more nervous.

Pierre (in an expensive suit), Jules (disguised as a 50-year old woman), and Max, all carried badges from the Swiss Financial Market Supervisory Authority, in charge of financial regulation.

* * * *

Max and Jules strolled into the bank far ahead of Pierre, who was studying every face on the street as he lollygagged behind the siblings.

Across the grand entrance, Max strode directly but casually to the Manager's office, showing his badge, flashing his handsome smile, and asking, "Can he speak to me, or do I need an appointment?"

He knew any bank with an investigator in the office would never turn them away. That alone often had legal ramifications.

Jules watched with a half-smile as she mostly watched the people around them. Nobody seemed to know anything at all was out of the ordinary.

"Ms. Corday," she heard Max using her new name.

She followed him into the manager's office.

* * * *

They exited the office and walked out, followed closely by Pierre.

Once in the car, Jules gave Pierre a thumbs up.

Max waited a few beats before saying to anybody who might be listening by now, "They are in compliance. Nothing here."

BOOTS BEGIN THE DANCE

February 15, 2016; Prague, Czech Republic

Sopranov and Orlov met Mantribe at the lake house the French spies were listening to.

They greeted each other as the old friends they now were, but Sopranov and Orlov had a message to deliver.

* * * *

Over drinks on the balcony – to which the French had added a mic since that first meeting they snooped on – Sopranov cleared his throat.

"Sorry to bring you here like this."

"No worries," Mantribe said. "Tell me what's the matter."

"The president is a little worried about our candidate," Sopranov eased into it.

* * * *

As Mantribe laid out the campaign dynamics for his clients, Sopranov and Orlov nodded at the appropriate moments.

When Mantribe stopped, Sopranov nodded, smiling.

"The president wants you in campaign," Sopranov said in a no-nonsense voice. "Actively in the campaign."

"This because of Iowa?"

Woody had come in a close second in Iowa.

"Only partly," said Orlov.

"But enough," Sopranov said. "He's nervous. Would feel better with you on campaign plane."

"Understood," Mantribe assured them.

"He wants you to be campaign manager," said Sopranov conspiratorially.

"That would be tricky – could even backfire on us."

Sopranov shrugged. "We also need to put a DSN line on a server at Felix's place in Woody's Worldwide. And one in Michigan."

"It'll hook up the campaign and my bank, like a digital hotline connecting us and, shutting out the rest of the world – designed to obscure its own existence."

Mantribe looked impressed.

"We can talk over it?"

Orlov nodded. "And email over it, transmit money over it. Michigan is only other place we need this."

"I'll see to it."

Before they left Prague, Mantribe agreed to get a top job in Woody's campaign. Just not campaign manager.

February 18, 2016; Moscow, Russia, Upscale Restaurant

Pierre sat alone appearing to read a book. The unseen earbud, however, let him eavesdrop on a top Tutin adviser who'd already had way too much to drink.

The advisor was not known for frequenting hookers, so the woman he was with was most likely a date.

Pierre cocked his head slightly. This might be useful.

"This is Russia's time on the world stage," the advisor bragged. "We have something in the information arena which will allow us to talk to the Americans as equals."

February 29, 2016

Early voting began in Florida, although voters had been mailing in ballots for weeks.

The insurrection's boots had already cast their mail-in ballots in the Michigan Democratic Primary.

March 1, 2016; Georgetown, Grand Cayman

The small plane carrying Jules, Max and Champion touched down at the Owen Roberts Airport.

"If, for any reason we get separated, come back to this airport, this plane," Champion said.

"Pilot's topping off fuel and filing a new flight plan. We close the door and taxi out as soon as we are all on board. Driver's a cop; will drive us straight to the plane."

"I'm worried about bullets now," Jules said bluntly.

"I know, the Russians are on to us," said Max evenly. "I'm a little nervous, too, but I remember about the breathing. I'm wearing body armor and a gun. Just peed. Think I'm good."

"Glad you are nervous," Jules said. "Use it. Do not be overconfident. Don't deviate from the plan.

* * * *

Jules and Max walked into a cavernous bank building, as Max pulled the same stunt he did in Zurich.

This time, however, Max was in disguise, with graying hair and a trim beard, and using a confident British accent, his Georgia drawl nonexistent.

Bank Security Office

A bank security officer picked up a phone. "We have an investigator here."

* * * *

"Ms. Abbott," said Max, using another name for his sister.

"Yes, sir," she said, following him into the manager's office.

* * * *

The bank manager escorted them to a private room with terminals in it. Jules reached into her purse and activated a camera/microphone jammer, since they were certain they'd be watched.

As Max stuck a drive into one of the terminals, data began downloading.

Bank Security Office

"We have a situation like you described," said the security officer looking at a terminal. "An investigator is here and downloading files. They have proper documents."

He paused.

"Very well."

* * * *

Finished with the download, Max gave it to Jules who efficiently shoved the drive into a pocket under her body armor.

Walking out, Max thanked the manager, "Everything is compliant," Max assured him, shaking his hand.

Before they could clear the lobby, a security officer asked them to stop. Every nerve was on the outside of Jules' body. All she could focus on was keeping Max safe.

"May I see your credentials again, Mr. Anderson?" the guard asked.

Pulling them out, Max appeared to be unruffled and relaxed. But his pulse was racing.

Jules put her hand in her purse to get her finger on the trigger of her gun.

The guard looked at them unhappily and frowned. "Please remain here," he said.

Max looked at his watch, annoyed. "How long please? We have a heavy schedule."

"I don't know," he said abruptly.

Jules released the gun in her purse and removed her phone, pretending to make a call. "Do you have service?" she asked Max, telling him with her eyes that something was wrong.

"Maybe closer to a window or door," she said, moving toward the door.

His phone out, Max was following Jules' lead.

Jules touched her broach to tell Champ they may have been made.

Outside, Champion felt a vibration on the disk under his belt. He drew his gun, removing the safety as he said to the driver, "Engines on, we may be blowing out of here." He stepped outside the car.

Suddenly, Champion's attention was drawn to a familiar-looking man. He'd seen him before in Russia. Although he was Armenian, he was a Russian assassin. Champion touched the disk under his belt to tell Jules danger was lurking.

* * * *

Jules felt the vibration and said into the phone to nobody, "O.K., we will be right there."

* * * *

Champion saw them exit the building and he drew a bead on the Armenian assassin. Suddenly, the Armenian dropped out of sight.

Champion turned around, opened the back door and shouted, "Head down – RUN!" He kept looking for the Armenian, using the car and the open door for cover.

Holding Max's hand, Jules ran the few yards to the car, diving in first as bullets began hitting all around. One hit Max in the body armor, knocking him away from the door.

Champion left his place of some protection to go after Max, as Jules popped back out to cover them, returning automatic fire.

Max recovered fast and lunged into the backseat, as a bullet hit Champion in the leg.

Hearing the sickening thud, Jules ducked out and grabbed his belt, pulling his arm over her shoulder. She pushed him into the back seat.

Max pulled Champion across the back seat, himself on the floor.

Jules jumped in and slammed the door, yelling "GO!" as the bullet proof glass broke, protecting the team from the last bullet. But the driver hadn't needed the instruction, peeling out as soon as Jules' body was inside.

She inspected the amount of blood loss. It wasn't

gushing, a very good sign, but it was bleeding badly.

Climbing into the front seat to ride shotgun, she reloaded, saying, "How bad, Champ?"

"Not so bad," he said through clenched teeth. "Not squirting, don't think it got an artery."

"Maxie, sit under his leg and elevate it straight up," she said. "Put pressure on the wound."

Max quickly complied. Champion moaned, wincing.

As the car sped away, a police chase began. The car, riddled with bullets sped to the airport.

"Talk to me, Max, how's the bleeding?"

Max, holding Champion's leg against his chest, said, "The bleeding might have slowed down a little bit. But he needs a hospital."

"No," Champion chimed in. "We've got a med kit on the plane. Staying is more dangerous."

* * * *

Arriving at the plane, engines already running, Max and Jules carried Champion up the stairs.

"Stairs up, wheels up," Jules ordered as her foot left the stairs. "We got wounded."

Laying Champion down on the couch, she spun back to help the co-pilot pull in the stairs as the plane moved toward the runway. She closed the door and sealed the air lock.

"Buckle up," said the pilot. "We are number one for takeoff."

"Maxie, tie him in," Jules said, running to the galley. Coming back with a medical bag, a straw and Gatorade, she sat down quickly and buckled herself in as the plane began speeding for takeoff.

The airplane ascended into the afternoon sky.

Jules dug into the medical bag and said gently, "Can you talk to me Champ?"

"Getting woozy, but still OK. If the Armenian'd gotten an artery, I'd be dead," Champion said softly.

"You always know what to say to the chicks, Champ. Maxie," she handed him the Gatorade and straw. "Get this in him, I'm a little worried about his fluids. Soon as we level out, elevate his leg again."

Digging into the medical bag, Jules said happily, "Hey, there's a banana bag here."

As the plane leveled out, Jules unbuckled the seatbelt and went to Champion. "I'll elevate the leg again, you get him out of the coat and shirt," she said to Max.

They went about tending to Champion.

Max watched with awe and wonder as his little sister – with no trepidation whatsoever – inserted the needle into Champion's vein and attached the IV bag.

"So Jules Bond is also a doc?" Max asked.

"Battlefield tactics," she smiled. "Be surprised how much non docs can do when you need medical attention."

Hand on Champion's head, stroking him gently, she said, "We do need to get you to a hospital. IV buys us a little time, but not that much. Wanna land in Miami? "

"No, please not Miami."

"How about Atlanta?" Max offered.

"Max, the Russians are chasing us," Champion winced. "Their mafia is everywhere. Including Atlanta."

"Yeah, but we know people there."

Jules looked like she was weighing risks. Finally, she spun to go to the cockpit to place a secure call.

South of Atlanta, Georgia; Atlanta South Regional Airport

About 20 miles south of Atlanta, the private jet landed and came to a stop at three emergency vehicles, two police cars and an ambulance.

"When your Daddy's the sheriff …" Max gestured at the flashing lights, smiling with relief.

Seeing her father standing on the tarmac with two paramedics, Jules smiled and popped the air lock, opened the door and lowered the stairs.

Sheriff Archer entered the plane first, followed by the paramedics with a gurney.

Kissing his daughter, he said to the pilot behind her, "Need to top off fuel?"

"No sir, we are good to get to Andrews."

"Very well, I told the tower you'd either need a quick turnaround or a top off first."

March 2, 2016; Bethesda, Maryland, Naval Medical Center

Post-surgery, Champion was sacked out, his leg bandaged. Sheriff Archer snored softly in the chair beside his bed.

Jules stood behind Max at a laptop, showing Zack the data they'd stolen.

"Way to go, Maxie," Zack patted him on the back, smiling.

March 8, 2016; Michigan's primary

Pre-election polling had shown Clanton with a significant lead in Michigan's Democratic Primary.

But Ernie Banders took the lead as early returns came in, eventually winning by two percentage points. The boots had drawn blood.

The story of the Michigan election became about Clanton's inherent weakness, not Sanders' strengths. Just as the Russians had planned and hoped.

Woody won the Republican nomination easily over the remaining two opponents in the Republican race.

Moscow, Russia, The Kremlin, Tutin's office

Orlov, Sopranov and Tutin exchanged smiles when the results out of Michigan were announced.

Seeing Clanton looking unhappy in defeat, Tutin pumped a clinched fist in victory.

Sopranov poured expensive vodka in three shot glasses, the men clinked the glasses and drank.

"We're gonna win," Tutin said, feeling more confident in the insurrection again.

"We're gonna win, no matter who they elect," Sopranov purred.

PRIMARIES

March 12, 2016

Social media trends in Michigan showed a giant uptick in Russian-sponsored fake news supporting Woody.

March 15, 2016; Florida

On Primary Election Day, Florida experienced various malfunctions in their voter registration system.

Scenes repeated themselves all over the state.

A voter standing at the check in, looked confused.

"But I've been a registered Republican all my life. Please check again."

"I'm so sorry ma'am. You are welcome to cast a provisional ballot. If we can confirm your affiliation, we will count the ballot."

A Republican observer approached the representative from the Elections Office. "What's going on?"

"This is happening all over the state," said the Elections Officer. "Happening big in Volusia, Duval, Orange, Palm Beach, Apopka, and Miami-Dade. Voters are being turned away from the polls by the hundreds because their party affiliation is 'NO PARTY.'"

Baffled, the Republican observer mouthed, "What?"

Miami, Florida, Dash Rock's home

Dash smiled a shit-eating grin.

The Florida pre-election polls had shown Woody leading the home state senator, Marco Rubio, 36% to 30%, within the margin of error.

The Russian boots had drawn blood a second time. Their 100,000 votes in Florida's Republican primary lifted Woody over Rubio, 46% to 27%.

March 21, 2016

Russian boots began early voting in Wisconsin.

March 29, 2016, Woody Presidential Plane

Kent Mantribe, who had been traveling with Dale Woody, officially joined the campaign as Convention Manager, tasked with lining up delegates.

Mantribe, Rock and Felix Slater sat in seats facing each other, heads close together.

Mantribe asked Rock, "Are you worried the 'No Woody' campaign will get strong enough to stop us?"

"It's a campaign, I'm worried about everything," Rock said absently, reading a memo. "Not the least of which is the Speaker, an opponent, is our convention chairman."

They were worried for good reason. Republicans weren't yet ready to give up their souls.

April 3, 2016; London, England, Jules' Flat

When Jules opened her front door to go running, Tiny (the Great Dane) scrambled out to clear the hallway.

Jules reached down to pick up the newspaper.

She smiled. "OK, Maxie, here's info we didn't have to steal."

The *Guardian's* headline was: *"Global Laundromat of Rich Russians."*

The Panama Papers were now public. A global collaboration of journalists from more than 80 countries had found the hidden wealth of some prominent world leaders – revealed by an unprecedented leak showing how the rich exploit secretive offshore tax regimes.

Jules ran her finger down the story till she found it.

"According to the Corruption Reporting Project nearly $21 billion was pumped out of Russia by suspected criminals in Russia via accounts in Latvia and Moldova at banks notorious for their exposure to money-laundering scams – between January 2011 and October 2014.

Around 500 people are thought to have been involved in the money-laundering operation. These include oligarchs, Moscow bankers and figures working for or connected to the FSB, the successor spy agency to the KGB."

Jules tossed the paper into her apartment as Butch (the German Shepherd), finally came out, ready for the morning run.

She took off smiling.

April 5, 2016

Wisconsin's primary was open, meaning voters could choose to vote in either primary.

Despite the boot's 100,000 votes for Woody in the Republican primary, Woody lost the primary by three points. But their numbers did make it appear there were over 60,000 more U.S. voters casting ballots for Republicans in Wisconsin than in previous elections, a highly unusual anomaly.

April 20, 2016

A story on the front page of the *New York Times* was headlined: *"Kent Mantribe Named Woody's Campaign Manager."*

April 26, 2016

On CNN, results flashed from the Pennsylvania Republican Primary.

Woody – who was heavily favored – won big.

Likewise, Clanton, heavily favored in the Democratic primary, won handily.

Over 440,000 more Pennsylvanians voted in the Democratic primary than the Republican Primary, even with the boots weighing in with 100,000 Republican votes there.

May 4, 2016; Moscow, Russia, Outdoor Park

Pierre sat reading a Russian paper, but listening to a conversation nearby.

Pierre was particularly interested in the pair of spies – one of whom was a well-known Russian military intelligence officer – he'd casually followed here.

These were the gigs that generally produced nothing useful, but when they did produce something, it was usually a doozy.

"Russia is about to take our rightful place as first among nations," the Russian military intelligence officer bragged to a colleague as they had a sandwich.

"Our influence campaign in Great Britain is gaining traction," he said conspiratorially. "We may be able to move the vote there to get Britain to leave the European

Union – that weakens NATO and the west. That's not even our best effort."

"President Tutin will soon pay back that bitch Clanton for the influence operation she ran against him in 2011," he smiled wickedly.

"How?" asked the colleague, taking it all in – as was Pierre, seemingly unaware, 20 feet away.

"We are going to cause chaos in the upcoming U.S. election with an influence campaign of historic scope, and even intervene in the voting. They won't know what hit them, who did it, who to believe about it."

"That's the key to destabilizing NATO for us. We can control the European continent."

"Exactly. Ocean to ocean."

* * * *

Pierre opened his laptop. Opening an email, he wrote: "Attached wiretap between Russian military intelligence officer and colleague at lunch. First indication that Russia is not just hacking email accounts, but could be interfering with the U.S. voting in 2016."

May 5, 2016; Washington, D.C., FBI Headquarters

"Oh shit," said Director Cummings, reading the text of the conversation, as Zack danced nervously in the Director's office, but tried to stand still at the same time.

"CIA's seen it?"

"Yes sir," Zack said quickly. "Director made raw intel into an official report and circulated it. Even added it to the Presidential Daily Brief."

Zack's nervous energy began to spill over a little.

"I don't know if this is the worst part or not …

nobody knows what to do."

"This is the first mention of actual meddling in our voting?"

"That we've heard, yes. So it could be a head fake."

"If Russia's intention is to undermine western democracies – including this one – doesn't it make more sense to make us worry about that, waste manpower and energy chasing shadows? It would give great cover to whatever they are actually doing."

"It would."

Zack nervously tapped the director's desk. "A CIA officer and a family member who's a banker, have stolen pertinent records from banks in Switzerland and the Caymans. They've shared the information with the task force, but not the records. We were right on target. Russia is behind the money going into fake companies and shells there, and coming here – often to political accounts."

"So nothing we can use in a prosecution."

"What about RICO? That gives us wide berth."

The Racketeer Influenced and Corrupt Organizations Act, shorthanded as 'RICO,' was passed in 1970 to have a structure for police to control international mob crime in the United States.

"RICO?" the director thundered.

He looked at Zack incredulously. He pushed back from his desk. The director pursed his lips, as he always did when trying to make a big decision.

He stood up suddenly.

"You'd RICO a political candidate or party as we go into the general election? Jesus, Zack."

Zack looked down, eyes closed tight. He knew this was a long shot.

"That also makes the investigation public," Zack added quietly, not that helpfully. "More people we question, word can get out."

"When can we catch a damn break on this?" Director Cummings lamented. "An election year is the worst time for an investigation, or even word of an investigation."

Zack knew what else was weighing on the Director. Not the time to press him on this. He changed direction.

"Is there any clarity to the Clanton email stuff?"

"Aw, she's cocky and private. She was a little careless with badly marked classified matters, but not criminal. Not sure how to proceed, but we're done with that part."

"Twelve congressional committees doing proctology reports on her and all they get for their trouble is 'a little careless?' Congress makes me want to vomit."

"Here's the tricky part. In the last document dump, one of Russia's edited emails included an off topic sentence. That General Lynch was going to get Secretary Clanton off."

"Shit," Zack breathed out. "But they know it's fake, right?"

"I don't know! My guess is they seize on it and say, 'see, the fix was in for her.'"

"But it's a *fake* document," Zack said.

"Yes. I. Know," the Director spit. "I'm saying that won't matter to these guys in Congress now. Fake or not, they'll investigate the living shit out of it. I need to beat them to the punch, and without General Lynch. Try to hold on to some semblance of law … and evidence."

June 7, 2016; Riverside County, California

The Riverside District Attorney opened the door to his office beside a clock reading 7:35. His phone was ringing off the hook. Dropping his briefcase at the door, he tripped into his desk, spilling his coffee.

"Shit," he said, reaching for first line on his desk phone. "DA's office, hang on," he repeated until the ringing stopped and went back to the first line, pushing the speaker button.

"How can I help you?" he said, opening a drawer for towels to clean up the coffee.

"I can't vote," the woman's voice said. "Somebody changed my registration." He looked confused.

That conversation repeated itself many more times in his office, and in the offices of county clerks, and state election officials around California.

June 24, 2016; London, England, Jules' Flat

In a sports bra, shorts and socks, Jules picked up her new passport.

The face in the picture that stared back was her same face, but not.

Gone were her trademark long dark locks. Her hair was shorter now, dyed either blonde, white, or red. Shorter hair made use of wigs easier — and offered the option of a disguise as a boy.

In the passport, her hair was blonde.

She examined the pronounced scar on her left temple where her head slammed against the side of her plane in the escape from Russia.

Her new name and nationality: Julianna Corday, of the United Kingdom.

As Jules put on her shoes to go running, with the dogs dancing in anticipation of the morning exercise, the TV announced results of the British referendum to leave the European Union, known as "Brexit."

"In a stunning, narrow decision that will have security, economic and political repercussions for decades to come, British voters have narrowly passed Brexit, initiating Britain's exit from the European Union," said the exhausted anchor.

Jules turned off the TV. She shook her head and muttered, "Russia, one. Good guys, zero."

One of the dogs made a whiney noise, anxious to get going.

"Let's go," she opened the door and Tiny went out first, her position when they ran. Butch ran behind Jules.

Long considered a joke, British leaders were surprised when Brexit got on the ballot.

The U.K. was leaving the European Union, the political and economic union that fully launched in 1993, whose sole purpose was to unify Europe.

Europe was largely slapped around in the 20th Century by two world wars and a decades-long Cold War.

The first Cold War played out roughly on western European stages, deadly in eastern European nations, and was punctuated by the Berlin Wall and a Soviet nuclear missile crisis in Cuba.

July 5, 2016

As the much-used "BREAKING NEWS" banner binged across the screen, CNN's anchor said, "*CNN has learned that the FBI has cleared presumptive Democratic nominee Hailey Clanton in an investigation into her use of a private email server during her time as secretary of state.*

The FBI Director will NOT recommend charges against Clanton, but did say that Clanton and her aides were 'extremely careless' in handling classified information."

July 6, 2016

Another batch of hacked DNC documents appeared on the Guccifer 2.0 website, a site affiliated with Russian intelligence.

Illinois Board of Elections

A part time contractor looked at the screen in front of him and cocked his head. That was wrong. He began typing.

He picked up a phone. "I'm watching unauthorized data leaving the network. It looks like hackers got access to the state's voter database."

The database contained names, dates of birth, genders, driver's licenses and partial Social Security numbers on 15 million people, half of whom were active voters.

July 15 2016; Cleveland, Ohio, Republican Convention

Dash Rock greeted Russian Ambassador Stepan Kozlov on the hotel rooftop, hugging his old friend.

"Stepan, get in here – you know Marc Glenn." General Marc Glenn and Ambassador Kozlov hugged as the old friends they now were.

"These are some of the other members of our campaign national security advisors," Rock gestured to a woman and three men in suits whose bearing screamed former military.

"Sit. What are you drinking?"

* * * *

"Every time we talk about national security, Woody

always leads off with wanting to improve relations with Russia, Mr. Ambassador," said General Glenn earnestly. "Our priority going forward is to work closely with Russia as an ally and a friend."

"What of a NATO mention in the platform?" the Ambassador asked pleasantly. The platform was the governing policy document for the campaign, to be judged by voters in the coming election.

For the first time in the history of party conventions and their party platforms, a major political party was negotiating with a foreign adversary on a plank in their policy commitments.

"We're looking at doing two things during the campaign," Rock said. "We're going back to hitting the Europeans for not paying up on defense, and questioning the need for NATO at this point in history."

"In terms of the platform – we want to remove the Republican Party's support for the Ukrainian resistance in 2014 against Russia," Glenn outlined the agreement gently. "I know that's important to your country – immediately – and our conversations through the summer and fall will make it possible for us to step away from NATO and Article Five of the charter."

Article Five of the North American Treaty Organization (NATO) guaranteed the right of mutual protection, an all-for-one deal for military protection if any of the members were ever attacked. That alone did more to contain Soviet – and later Russian – aggression in Europe than anything else.

The only time Article Five was invoked was by the United States, after the 9-11 attacks in 2001.

Every European ally then rallied to the defense of the U.S., including Turkey, NATO's only Muslim member.

July 17, 2016; Washington, D.C., FBI Headquarters

Zack closed the door behind him, walking quickly to the head of the table.

"We have some new people here today. Max Archer, a former banker who's a CIA asset." He gestured to Jules, "Julianna Corday, former chief of Moscow station. She had to run after Snowden gave them her name. She's the one who stole back a couple of drives Snowden gave the spy academy."

Other members of the team, from CIA, to NSA to FBI technology specialists – about 20 altogether – nodded at her in awe.

A piece of Snowden's cache of information being stolen back from Moscow was now legendary.

"There are two other members of this team, Steve Champion in London and Pierre Montesquieu in Moscow. Julianna, Max, Champ and I are the only ones in touch with Pierre. The Soviets are all over him, so we talk when he can."

Pointing to a man whose bearing screamed scientist, Zack said, "We've been working with RAND researcher, Dr. Danny Varela, formerly at DARPA." (Defense Advanced Research Projects Agency, at DOD, develops emerging technologies for the military.)

"Most of what we know about the techniques and methods of social media propaganda comes from a program Danny created to study how dictators might manipulate social media in the future."

Zack paused, set his jaw, and changed paths.

"The Director is not ready to go public with this, and not ready to RICO anybody yet," Zack conceded. "What's the art of the possible here?"

"There *is* a path for RICO," said one of the FBI task

force members.

"Yes," said Zack, pointing at him. "You and the financial team focus exclusively on that."

"Let's separate out things in terms of what we know, what we can prove in court, what we think, and what evidence we can take to Congress and the court of public opinion," Zack said.

* * * *

"Danny's algorithms were a part of what Snowden gave the Russians," Zack said. "That's helped us in a couple of ways. We've followed their work easier, and undermined it in real time where we've seen it. But that's like dipping water out of the ocean with a spoon."

"They stole our own propaganda weapon?" asked another task force member.

"Snowden stole it from a contractor and gave it to them," Zack frowned. "A weapon, by the way, we have never employed."

"The Russians are 10 years ahead of us in being willing to make use of social media to influence public opinion," Varela said.

Like many Jewish families, Varela's grandparents fled Europe in 1938 as Hitler began to advance. They believed they'd merely be avoiding a war.

Instead, they saved themselves from the Holocaust.

Thanks to that inspired decision on the part of his forefathers, Danny was here today to talk of similar, but even more frightening, global propaganda efforts than Hitler's.

"In the Cold War, spies spread disinformation to targeted political groups," Varela said.

"Now they harness computing power to segment and

target literally millions of people in real time online. That's how the Russians can potentially change behavior on the scale of democratic governments."

"We just watched them do it in the U.K. on Brexit," Jules shook her head sadly.

The heart rate of each person in the room increased. All looked at Danny with fear and doubt.

"They couldn't do that here," snorted Max.

"They already have," Danny said. "Here's how they are doing it – social media manipulation and hacking."

"Illinois is our 'Patient Zero' in what will be a hacking pandemic that we've seen them do in other countries," Danny said. "They hacked into California's central voter-registration database, but they didn't record the event."

"With evidence from the Illinois data banks, we've developed digital signatures, and protocol addresses used by the attackers so we can see the hackers in real time."

"Homeland Security is sending these signatures and alerts to every state," he continued. "Got 37 states with traces of the hackers. In Florida and California, hackers were in systems that make an electronic voter ID system used by poll workers."

"In Illinois, hackers tried but failed to alter or delete some information in the database," Danny said ominously. "This ain't just a spying mission."

THE SOVIET CANDIDATE

July 18, 2016; Cleveland, Ohio

The *Washington Post* headline read:
"Woody Campaign Guts Ukrainians' Resistance to Russia's 2014 Invasion"

Story read: *"The Woody campaign worked behind the scenes in Cleveland, ahead of the Republican Convention, on a plank of the 2016 Party Platform that gutted the GOP's longstanding support for Ukrainians' popular resistance to Russia's 2014 invasion."*

* * * *

Later that day, Russian Ambassador Stepan Kozlov passed a sign in the hotel, *"21st Century Foreign Policy, hosted by the Heritage Foundation."*

"Mr. Ambassador!"

Kozlov turned to see the senator from Alabama, who had been the first sitting senator to jump on the Woody bandwagon. The Senator, a former district attorney, was always amenable to helping friends who helped his campaign committee.

That made the Alabama Senator no different, really, than any other Member of Congress. This was so easy, Kozlov thought.

"Senator, thank you so much for your help with the policy committee last night on the Ukrainian language," the ambassador charmed.

The Senator, eternally grateful for the campaign help he'd gotten from lobbyists associated with Ukraine – Mantribe among them – glad-handed the Ambassador.

"Happy to help," the Senator drawled. "We agree about so much – the Cold War is over and we can be economic allies now. Ukraine just isn't our problem."

Ever so grateful for the decade-long influence campaign in the U.S., Kozlov's smile lit up his round face, remembering the evening before.

A fight over the party's platform language supporting the Ukrainian resistance got pretty heated, but the presumptive nominee showed the Russians his word was good in terms of doing their bidding on official Republican policy.

Woody's guys on the policy committee removed all reference to support for the Ukrainian resistance.

Now it was a matter on which all Republicans would run and be judged. That made many elected Republicans very nervous, sensing a coming choice between Russia and NATO.

But that was really beyond this election.

Woody wasn't going to win anyway.

July 22, 2016; 10:30 am EDT

WikiLeaks released Russia's trove of Democratic National Committee emails – selectively edited.

All told, WikiLeaks was Russia's conduit for making public 44,053 emails with 17,761 attachments from the DNC, from and about the top Democratic lawmakers, staffers, contributors and – most significantly – the presidential candidate and her top command.

It was a devastating and humiliating release with

enough information to keep reporters busy and entertained all the way to Election Day, as America's free press unknowingly collaborated with the Russian manipulation campaign.

Just as Russia and the cabal had scripted it.

July 27, 2016; Doral, Florida, Woody Press Conference

Standing before an adoring crowd – his preferred medium – Woody assailed his Democratic opponent as the Democrats tried to put out their general election message while battling daily stories about emails stolen from the DNC, edited by Russia, and amplified by all levels of the news ecosystem as though they were real.

Then Woody veered wildly off message, even for him.

"Russia, if you're listening, I hope you're able to find the 30,000 emails that are missing. You will be rewarded mightily by our press."

Responding to a reporter's question, Woody insisted: "I never met Tutin. I've never spoken to him."

Moscow, Russia; State Russian intelligence office

Most people around the world watched in bemused horror as Woody invited Russian hackers to attack the U.S. Justice Department – and the private email server at the Clanton home in upper New York – to find anything criminal looking.

At the office Nikoly Orlov kept at the state intelligence central headquarters, he and Sopranov watched in much the same way.

Each man shook his head.

"What the fuck?" Sopranov whispered quietly, his hand open, palm up in confusion.

"Stupid idiot," Orlov said just as quietly.

"Vad said 'useful idiot,'" Sopranov corrected him playfully, invoking the president's derisive term.

Orlov acknowledged that with a smile and nod.

Sopranov paused, shrugged, and then said, "Well, he got performance bonus."

July 28, 2016; Washington, D.C., FBI Headquarters

Director Commings' tall frame ducked into the room.

Several people on phones saw the boss come in and said, "I'll call you back." And "Gotta go."

"Hey, sorry to interrupt you guys."

The director looked around at the team of now several dozen agents from the FBI, CIA, and NSA investigating collusion between members of the Woody campaign and Russian operatives.

"Time to formally change the focus and name of this task force," Commings said. "The Snowden Task Force is now the Russian 2016 Election Task Force. You're still investigating what the Russians are planning to do to the election, and any collusion between the Woody campaign and Russian operatives."

Zack interjected, "Boss, this is the most vexing search. Because it's politics, it's freedom of speech, advocacy. They're dropping fake documents, fake videos everywhere."

The director slumped in defeat.

"I felt jerked around by the Russians, the Democrats, and the Republicans in Congress on the whole Clanton email deal. Hate that we needed to do that publicly because we know Russia has a fake document – and that Congress won't care if it's fake."

"I gotta tell you I'm overwhelmed at our predicament

here," he said. "Russia is planning to intervene in the general election, the foundation of our democracy. If they can do that here, they can do it anywhere, with impunity."

"Bad enough Congress is so impotent," said Jules.

The director shrugged. That was part of what pulled at him.

"Here's the deal," he said. "Democracy's in deep shit. Only the people here can find the scheme, prove it, and get word to the American people before early voting begins."

They all knew exactly when early voting would begin, but so far were short of the information they needed for Grand Jury indictments.

"I'm not kidding, nearly 250 years of democracy depends on you getting to the truth. Shitty deal, I know, but there it is.

"Boss, we're still doing this in the shadows – no warrants, no grand juries," Zack said. "The influence campaign we can see more of every day. The right won't believe it and the left won't shut up if we go public."

"Monumentally shitty deal. I did bring something for your wall. I really need you guys to come through on this." With that, the Director spun and left.

The page he left for them in the bullpen of the task force said simply: "Your mission, should you decide to accept it: SAVE DEMOCRACY!"

July 31, 2016

Suddenly, the Woody campaign was under siege for their pro-Russian attitude.

Mantribe denied knowing anything about the platform change. Then Woody's Russian-born adviser spouted the Kremlin's party line, telling CNN: "Russia did not seize

Crimea. That's not what happened."

Washington, D.C., FBI HQ; Russian- Election Task Force

"How do you want to follow this?" Zack asked the Deputy Attorney General.

"It's important not to do it differently, just because it's politics," she said slowly. "On the other hand-"

"On the other hand, it's the first time I have really seen a high crime in action," said Jules. "If he's close in November, they might be able to swing it in some Democratic states with just the influence campaign."

"The president wants our response in line with past cyberattacks – despite the extraordinary political attack," said the Deputy AG, ironically, another Georgian.

"So this is the same as China stealing intellectual property, or Iran fooling with our financial institutions, or North Korea in the Sony attack?" Zack said.

"Wait," said Jules. "We've got Russians bragging about unleashing chaos on Election Day. What if the California and Illinois breeches were test runs for hackers in November?"

An uncomfortable silence followed. "Let us not forget," Jules said gently. "Russia's primary goal is to undermine public faith in the U.S. democratic process."

"Suppose their plan works," Max finally said. "There's no do over in our elections. That's it."

"Barring impeachment," the Deputy AG added.

"Yeah, but impeachment takes a real Congress. We haven't had that since 2010," Max sneered.

Her eyes narrowed, the Deputy AG weighed something in her head. Finally she turned to Jules.

"Do you really think Election Day tomfoolery is a possibility?" she asked.

"YES!" Jules said, exasperated. Hands together, pleading, she added, "Please, pass that up your food chain. Today, it's more certainty than possibility."

"Russia's tried this before, it didn't work then," said the Deputy AG.

"Our cyber guy says Moscow hacked the presidential campaigns in 2008 and 2012," Max smiled. "You'd see them, then poof, they're gone. This is a different game. More brazen. After 2014, we've found them in networks, and they'd stay, taunting us."

"But now," Jules punctuated her point with a finger. "They aren't just stealing shit to collect intelligence or to dump documents through Wikileaks. General, Russia intends to intervene in the voting itself, even if only to foul up the registrations in certain states."

Jules certainly had her attention.

The Deputy AG slumped as if she'd been shot.

"Elections aren't just counting ballots," the Deputy AG said slowly, shifting, trying to find her equilibrium. Her eyes locked on Jules as she sat forward. "It's how we know that the democratic will of the people is freely and fairly expressed."

"Yes," Jules said, not breaking the gaze.

Max was completely still, his eyes jumping back and forth between these two daughters of Georgia.

"For Russia, hacking that democratic consensus is a much easier reach," Jules said. She nodded at the Deputy AG as if to assure her this was the real deal.

"Russia can now erode the confidence of millions of voters, which – in itself – undermines our free and fair elections."

The Deputy AG slowly sat back again and stared at the ceiling for a long moment. She finally faced Jules again and nodded in understanding.

"Got it. I'll pass it up."

Jules nodded in thanks.

August 1, 2016; Moscow, Russia, The Kremlin, Orlov's Office

In a secured meeting room off his office, Orlov poured tea for Sopranov and President Tutin.

"We learned much from the primary elections. Since then, our spies have gotten jobs in the offices in charge of elections in our target states, in the areas with the largest numbers of Democratic voters," Orlov said proudly.

"We have designed malware for voting machines, which will shift five percent of the vote to Woody. Malware is designed to remain inactive during pre-election tests, activate itself when the polls open, stop when voting ends, and then delete itself, leaving no sign."

Smiling and rubbing his hands together in glee, Sopranov let out a whistle.

Smiling back, Orlov said, "We will use this only on Election Day, to minimize any discovery."

"How do you introduce malware?" Tutin asked.

"Just before each election, poll workers copy the ballot design from a regular desktop computer in a government office, and use jump drive to load the ballot onto each machine," Orlov explained. "Initial computer is never well secured, so malware can ride along with the ballot being loaded into voting machines."

Tutin laughed. He was feeling increasingly confident this might actually work.

"Fucking Americans. So rich. So addicted. So manipulated. More opportunities. Still they lose."

"One fact remains. It doesn't matter who wins. Look what they are doing to each other," Sopranov bragged, turning on the TV. "This is live."

Woody's face came up on the screen at a rally.

* * * *

At the same moment, on the other side of the planet in Columbus, Ohio, Woody went on the offensive, saying "I'm afraid the election is going to be rigged," to deliver the Kremlin line as the Republican nominee.

August 3, 2016; FBI's Russia-Election Task Force

Director Commings walked into the task force, tossing his briefcase on the chair by the door and striding to the large table in the center of the room.

"What's the feedback on this?" the director asked showing a paper with the headline: *"Homeland Security chief considering new cybersecurity for voting."*

"The right wing went nuts," Jules summarized.

"Ever since he proposed making voting systems 'critical infrastructure' – Russian bots are moving stories about a government takeover of elections, with Obama picking every president from now on," Zack said.

The FBI Director exhaled slowly, eyes closed, arms crossed. He finally stood up and stretched.

"If election systems were 'critical,' the administration gets more latitude to respond to a Russian cyberattack," the Director said. "There are 9,000 voting jurisdictions across the country."

"We've got a little evidence that they are trying to hack the vote in select voting machines," Jules said. "We've only got a scant theory that they are also using Russian spies to vote in the election – farfetched as it sounds."

"How the fuck do we cover all that?" asked another colleague

"Well, we're not going to need to," Zack said. "Republican-run states answered with a middle finger and a loud, 'fuck you;' we'll protect our own stuff."

"This is an unholy mess," said Jules, panicking. "Much as we have on these guys – almost *none* of it is stuff we can use in a prosecution. We're gonna need to go public soon. Americans cannot vote in the dark on this."

"How?" asked the Director. "What, exactly, do we say? We don't make public pronouncements absent a grand jury indictment."

Jules looked at the Director with a cold, incredulous stare, her mouth in a half-sneer.

"May I read the Clanton indictment?" she intoned clearly. "The one from the grand jury?"

"Jules that-" Zack tried to mitigate this, even accidentally calling her "Jules" instead of Julianna.

"I was in a terrible place," the Director said earnestly. "Secretary Clanton's arrogant as hell. She was a little careless with some classified stuff. That's not nothing."

"BUT – she's going to be elected, and we'll all still be here. I gotta live with that. Keeping the FBI out of the muck while both sides want us to investigate the other is a colossal task."

Jules spread her fingers out on the table in front of her, gathering herself. She was angry, but didn't want to respond in anger.

Zack looked on nervously.

"What if they are successful?" she asked quietly. "Can we all live with that? They've been at this since 2013 – that we know of. That's on top of the 2005-2012 influence campaign. We've only just begun to get a handle on the scope and full intentions."

She got up and paced for a minute.

"Even if we could eventually put this together at some

point during early voting, our only option would be to make a public pronouncement. Tick tock. The closer to the election, the less time our country has to absorb it."

"That's … my analysis," she said. "The only other option is for us to sit on this – never able to prosecute in a U.S. court, therefore, the American people not only have our democracy stolen, but they won't even know it!"

"There has to be some other way," Danny weighed in.

Nodding, the director looked appalled but felt guilty. She was right.

Pulling in his breath, he locked on her eyes.

"Not sure I can live with it if he wins," he said evenly but quietly. "Makes me nauseous just thinking about it."

He stopped and nodded at her, then at Zack and the other members of the team.

"Congress needs to know," said Jules gently.

"Yes, but I expect they will reject any alarm as instigated by Obama to swing the election to Clanton," said the Director. "That's their reflex. Nobody knows more about this than the people in this room."

He stood up. "Let's leave it at this today. You come up with a recommendation for how to proceed. Ms. Corday is right. But there are elements of this that can be segregated where a prosecution *is* still possible."

"Not without RICO for money laundering," said Zack. "We don't need the stolen bank info for that, we've been following Splater's money since 2013, along with Woody's, Mantribe's and Rock's. Been separate all along."

"Then include RICO in your recommendation," he tapped the wall. "Get off the mat and figure this out."

He walked out.

"Money laundering?" Max asked Zack, smiling.

August 8, 2016; Sochi, Russia, Olympic Village, Troll Farm

"I'M IN!" screamed one of the Russian hackers.

Orlov, standing close enough to hear, ran over. These geeks never got excited about anything.

"I just infiltrated the Florida election technology company again," the geek said, strutting.

"We phish for employees, one just swiped their log-in credentials," he explained excitedly. "Now I can imitate that employee and instruct local governmental officials about the election. Just need one."

"There's always one," Orlov high-fived the geek.

August 10, 2016; FBI's Russia Election Task Force

Director Commings carried in a Congressional letter. Handing it to Zack, he said, "Seen this?"

"Some House Democrats want us to investigate connections between Woody campaign guys and Russians who might have tried to interfere with the election."

"We have our recommendation. This half of the room," Zack waved at the math geeks and bankers – now including Max – "will focus on a racketeering operation, laying out the money going to Mantribe, Stone, Splater and Woody. Prepare a court case. Do what we do."

"This half," he gestured to the half of the room that included he, Jules, Danny Varela and geeks watching the cyber-attacks unfold and dig in, "Keeps looking for any way to prove electoral interference, and brief Congress."

"Make that brief in writing, make it easy to read," the Director said, knowing he may have to find a way to make it public.

"We already have it, sir," Jules said. "Best part, it's been prepared for months – in England, with Champion, who is the primary author. It's concise, mentions everything, and context is the western alliance."

She slid a single page over to Director Commings.

His eyes ran down the page. "This is good."

Unspoken was his delight that it was not an official FBI document. Somebody could release it when Congress refused to act in a bipartisan way in the face of a coordinated military attack on the nation.

The Director judged that now the Republicans *were* ready to part with their souls for the sake of this election.

For them it was all about keeping the majorities in the Congress, and an attempted theft of the majority on the Supreme Court.

They'd already operated outside the Constitutional parameters to deny the sitting president's Supreme Court nominee a hearing, much less a vote.

RUSSIAN SPIES AS VOTERS

August 15, 2016; Outside Moscow, Russia

For the better part of a year, Pierre laid out wiretaps anywhere one of the conspirators might pass and speak.

Tutin's team's obsessive care in not talking outside the confines of the Kremlin, or someplace equally secure, had kept the Russian's insurrection "boots" secret.

So many western spies had died or disappeared, Pierre was rarely communicating with the spy community in Moscow anymore – instead using the U.S. Defense attaché at the U.S. Embassy as a conduit if needed.

But Pierre was about to get lucky. Sitting in his car, across the street from a restaurant, Pierre watched Antony Sopranov eat with a lovely young lady in public.

He aimed his camera and shot several pictures.

He watched his Dutch partner, posing as the waiter, drop a mic in the pocket of Sopranov's jacket hanging on the back of his chair. Pierre's camera whirred, catching the moment.

* * * *

An hour later, Sopranov left the restaurant, planting a sloppy kiss and ass slap on the woman he'd shared breakfast with, jacket slung over his shoulder, feeling on top of the world.

Sopranov got into the back seat of a car.

Pierre followed them. The newspaper in the seat beside him was headlined: *Tutin to Leave on World Tour.*

* * * *

Sopranov's car drove into an underground garage of the Kremlin.

Pierre's heartbeat picked up. He turned around and parked so he could easily follow a car out of the garage.

Earbuds in, all he could hear was Sopranov breathing and the sound of him tapping out a text on his phone.

Suddenly, a door opening, the clatter of feet, and Sopranov greeted his old friend, Vadik Tutin.

* * * *

Inside the garage, the old friends embraced.

"Drive with me to my plane," the President said. Sopranov followed him, putting on his jacket.

* * * *

Earbuds in his ears and a smile on his face, Pierre pulled out well behind the President's entourage.

* * * *

Inside the presidential limo, the president was practically giddy.

"The Americans will never find our boots walking around among them," he said, believing the blocking device on the roof of his vehicle made the conversation secure.

But the disk in Sopranov's pocket was not blocked.

"Completely undetected in the primaries, and they will be just as undetected this fall," Sopranov bragged. "Vad, this is the best thing we ever did."

The president smiled.

"Woody will win the four states we focused on, Florida, Pennsylvania, Michigan and Wisconsin," Sopranov ran it down. "The Americans will shit if they ever realize how many ways we are fucking with their precious elections."

"With 100,000 extra votes getting cast and percentages getting moved to Woody through malware, the fix is in," the president said confidently.

"There are really only two questions remaining," Sopranov said. "Can the Americans discover us at all? And, of course, how will we celebrate on November 9?"

"Clanton will finally pay for what she did to us," the president said.

The men laughed as the procession of cars stopped alongside the presidential plane.

* * * *

Pierre, parked on the side of the road above the airport, watched the friends get out of the car, hug, and Sopranov get back in, as Tutin jogged up the stairs.

Pierre pulled out and drove directly to the pastry store behind the American embassy.

He sent an encoded message to the U.S. Defense Attaché.

* * * *

Minutes later, Pierre got in an SUV with the official.

"This is the most important evidence I've gotten yet

for our investigation," he said quickly, not handing the drive over just yet. "Too important to transmit on the usual channels."

Pierre paused. "What do you suggest?" he asked, although he knew what needed to happen.

"May I know what it is?" the Defense Attaché asked.

"I'm sorry, no. I've encrypted it. It is dangerous."

"Then I'll carry it there myself – now," the Defense Attaché said. "Where shall I land?"

"D.C.," Pierre said gratefully. "After you clear Russian airspace ask Zack Tolliver with the FBI to meet you."

August 16, 2016; Maryland, Andrews Air Force Base

As the Defense Attaché descended the stairs to the tarmac, Zack got out of the car beside the plane.

Shaking hands, he gestured they get in the car.

Punching a button to block surveillance, Zack asked, "What do you have?"

"I don't know," the Attaché replied. "But Pierre found me immediately after he recorded this, and encrypted it," he said, handing Zack the envelope Pierre'd given him with the drive and Pierre's handwritten note.

"I need to open this elsewhere," Zack said fast. "Can I drop you someplace?"

"No thanks," he answered. "Only delivering for our friend. You may need to get him out. Can't believe they haven't discovered him yet."

"You're right." Zack shook his hand. "May call you soon to help me do just that."

FBI Headquarters, Director's suite

"Whatdaya got?" Director Commings asked Zack.

Zack handed him the note.

The Director scanned Pierre's scrawl. "Z – for 4 eyes only. Segregate from other intel. Sensitive. R1 + R2. Got 'em!"

'Four eyes' was the intelligence community shorthand for the U.S. highest intelligence command: the President plus Directors of the CIA, National Intelligence, and the FBI.

"R1 is Tutin; R2 is Sopranov," Zack said, anxiously. "It's encrypted. You're one of the 'four eyes.' May I unencrypt it for you?"

"You think this is too sensitive for you to see Zack?"

"Pierre wouldn't restrict it otherwise. May I?"

The Director nodded.

Fingers running over keys, the screen began to alter itself.

Zack stood up before seeing it and walked to the other side of the laptop while the director put earbuds in his ears. He took them out immediately.

"It's a wiretap. In Russian. Which none of the four eyes speak. Get Julianna."

* * * *

Less than an hour later, Director Commings and Jules waited in the unusually empty White House Situation Room for the other three to arrive.

The President, CIA Director, and DNI (Director of National Intelligence) walked in together.

Before sitting down, the President put his hands on his hips, locked on Jules' eyes and said, "I count five pairs of eyes here."

"The tap is in Russian; this is Jules Archer," the Director intoned.

Jules looked at him quickly, realizing this was the rare room where everybody already knew she was still alive.

"Oh, right," she acknowledged. She looked at the CIA Director. "Hey, Boss." They shook hands across Director Commings.

The DNI smiled and pointed as if remembering. "Right, Chief of Moscow station."

The President patted her shoulder. "Welcome home."

"Yes sir … we, we can subtract my eyes. Here's," she pushed a single sheet of paper in front of the four, "the English transcript of the Russian you'll hear."

"Director Commings has several photographs taken by our French colleague still in Moscow. I'll be outside."

"You've already heard it," the president pointed at her chair. "Stay, please."

Nodding, she hit the tap, which played out the conversation in Russian, as the room read along. "Voices are Tutin and Sopranov."

T: Americans will never find our boots walking around among them.

S: Completely undetected in the primaries, and they will be just as undetected this fall.

S: Woody will win Florida, Pennsylvania, Michigan, Wisconsin. Americans will shit if they ever realize how many ways we are fucking with their precious elections.

T: With 100,000 extra votes getting cast, percentages getting moved to Woody through malware, election is over.

S: Two questions remain. Can the Americans discover us at all? How will we celebrate on Nov. 9?

LAUGHTER.

T: Clanton will finally pay for what she did to us.

"This was recorded yesterday by Pierre Montesquieu

from our task force in Moscow." She reached for the photos in front of Director Commings.

The first photo was of Sopranov in the restaurant with the woman over breakfast, the waiter's hand near Sopranov's jacket pocket.

"Not identified the woman, but that's a Dutch spy putting a listening device in his coat. Pierre followed Sopranov to the Kremlin where he rode with President Tutin to the airport."

"Conversation was in the car. Pierre encrypted it and took it to a confidant in the U.S. embassy, who hand-delivered it to Zack Tolliver, the head of our task force. With this note," she laid Pierre's original note in front of the President, who read it and moved it to the DNI.

"Zack gave me the note and drive, and unencrypted it, not knowing what it was. I got Agent-" he smiled, "Archer to translate for us on the ride here."

"Do you know why he restricted this to just us?" the President asked Jules.

"I don't. Except he got a treasure trove of info from the President and his money bags — and doesn't want to lose that limited access to Sopranov," Jules offered. "He wants to stay alive."

"We can't show this to the task force; it'll taint the investigation," Director Commings said.

"But *I'm* on the task force," Jules protested.

"You know how to do that," the CIA Director — her boss — reminded her.

She nodded, mouth tight.

"Can we find out why the agent restricted it?"

"Not until we talk to him," Jules said. "My guess, he's been running for a while. If he dies, restriction's off."

August 17, 2016, 7 a.m.; White House, Situation Room

The Four Eyes met alone to analyze options.

"No matter what we do, we can't stop Russia from giving the rest of the DNC's stuff, and other stolen emails, to WikiLeaks," said the DNI.

"Secretary Kerry called me last night," Director Commings said. "There's a spike in requests from Russia for temporary visas for people with IT skills to enter the U.S. for short-term assignments at Russian facilities."

"No visas before the election – and I want the entire fucking intelligence community all over this," the President said angrily as Commings nodded.

Obama looked at the DNI. "How does Moscow respond if we have some pre-election response to this?"

"This is unlikely to affect the outcome of the election," the DNI said quickly. "Russia might conduct a cyber-assault on voting systems on Election Day, throwing a Clanton victory into doubt."

The President breathed out loudly. "Woody is already predicting the election is rigged," he said slowly. "If we confirm it, don't we help Russia discredit the outcome and Hailey's presidency?"

Nobody said anything, but all three men nodded.

"Don't make things worse," the President said slowly. "Do three things now. Get a solid assessment on Russia's intent. Shore up vulnerabilities in state election systems. Get a *bipartisan* statement from Congress accusing Moscow, and urging states to take federal help."

"What-" the president stopped and walked to the door looking out into the Rose Garden. His hand tapped the door facing.

"So, what else can they do? Having spies here to vote multiple times is very bad. How the hell do we dig that out?" he asked.

"We cannot, legally – or even logistically – analyze every voter registration," the Director of National Intelligence/DNI said. "We've been worried about hacking, not spies here voting."

"Just so I can see the whole field – what else is possible for Russia to do?" Obama asked.

"They can slightly alter the voter rolls," said Director Commings. "Deleting records would be too obvious, but flipping a letter in every voter's address could mean every voter in a swing county would have to vote by provisional ballot. Gives Tutin a way to question our election integrity."

"They could post a video of hacking into a single voting machine and say, 'We did this to a hundred thousand machines across the country,'" said the DNI. "Just to sow doubt about every machine in the country, undermine our democratic credibility."

"They could interfere with the election reporting system," Director Commings said. "Our vote tally is decentralized and extremely slow – that's the system's strength. But on election night, nearly all reporting across all media platforms relies on the Associated Press. Altering AP's data, or taking down their system, could cause chaos."

"I feel like I can't quite breathe," the President said quietly. "Meet me back here for breakfast."

August 18, 2017, 7 a.m.; White House, Situation Room

The Four Eyes met again, albeit with food this time.

"We sent out flash alerts to states with the digital prints of the hackers we had got in Illinois and Arizona," Director Commings began as the President sat down.

"The Task Force realized last night that Russian hackers penetrated electoral systems in Florida and New Mexico, too," the DNI said. "In Tennessee, hackers clawed into the state's campaign-finance system."

"Shit," the President said softly.

"What most frightens my shop is we know we're seeing only Russia's clumsiest efforts," said the National Security Agency/NSA Director. The NSA collects global data for U.S. intelligence. "Orlov's hackers are the best in the world. We suspect they are everywhere and we just cannot see them."

"What's my first step, a warning?" Obama asked.

"Yes sir," said the CIA Director. "Minister to minister today. Follow up at the G20 in China in a couple of weeks to Tutin's face. Go from there."

September 4, 2016, Hangzhou, China, G20 Summit

President Barack Obama and the Russian President met privately, ostensibly to talk about the joint effort to combat ISIS in Syria.

But the U.S. President's eyes bored in on the smaller man, balancing charm and menace all at once.

"Your intelligence service is hacking into our election systems," Obama said bluntly. "Some things are fair game to try and hack, I guess. But not elections."

"Do not hack into the election processes of the world's oldest democracy."

"You lecture me about elections?" the Russian President said haughtily. "Do not dare. Stealing election from United States is like taking candy from baby."

He snarled, pivoted quickly and walked away.

"Americans will choose our own leaders," the U.S. President called after him. "We'll consider that an attack.

At least consider the ramifications of an attack on our homeland. We are not a former Soviet republic, Vad."

The Russian President waved his hand dismissively.

September 9, 2016; FBI's Russia Election Task Force

Only nine states asked Homeland Security to help secure machines at the polls, and for scans of online voter registration databases, ahead of the presidential election.

"Good news is the warning might be working," Danny said, pouring coffee for he, Zack and Jules. "For now."

"But we are going into this thing pants down," Jules began.

"And bent over, continuing the analogy," Danny said.

The Director walked in.

"This is how you'll brief Congress," the Director smiled. "Pants down, bent over?"

"No, no, of course not," Danny said, face reddening.

The Director nervously ran his hand over his head. "We don't have incontrovertible evidence. Zack, early voting begins in two weeks. We give 'em what we have."

"Take Max with you, since he's not an agent. If we need to refer to the money laundering side of this, I prefer he speak to that as a banker, a non-agent."

September 12, 2016; Washington, D.C., U.S. Capitol

In the Capitol's fourth floor secure briefing room, Zack, Jules, Max and Danny sat looking at Congress's "big eight" – including the Senate Majority and Minority leaders, the House Speaker and House Minority Leader, and the Chair and ranking members of the intelligence committees in the House and Senate.

Danny and Max handed out the single page document

to each person.

"I'll give you a couple of minutes to read and absorb the document, but will tell you while you read who compiled this," Zack said gently.

"A spy for Britain's MI6 in Moscow, Steve Champion, who now runs a private intelligence firm catering mostly to corporate clients, began hearing from Russian contacts and former colleagues about Russian intentions to interfere in our 2016 election."

Not a single eye looked up, as all eight sets of eyes sped hurriedly though the document, as Zack paused to let them read.

"Champion is the primary author of this dossier. It's everything known to western spies about Russian interference in the coming election."

DOSSIER – SECRET AND CONFIDENTIAL

Russian attempts to intervene in U.S. elections/2016
Candidate DALE WOODY/campaign associates
Collusion with Russia to destabilize 2016 elections

TUTIN AIMS TO DIVIDE NATO TO RETURN TO THEIR 19th-CENTURY 'GREAT POWER' POLITICS OVER THE DEMOCRATIC ORDER.

* Dutch, British, French and U.S. Intelligence agencies have heard multiple conversations in the last five years, all confirming that TUTIN repurposed his spy agency from battlefield operations to undermining western elections, as well as intervening in other western matters.

* These same Intelligence Community/**IC** Moscow assets uncovered massive influence campaigns underway in NATO nations. One in Britain, supporting referendum to exit the European Union. The other is in U.S., supporting

Dale Woody for president.
* Aim, endorsed by TUTIN, has been to encourage splits between U.S. and NATO, other western allies.

TUTIN ESTABLISHED PERSONAL LIAISON WITH WOODY TEAM FOR INTEL EXCHANGE IN 2011: ONGOING.

* TUTIN financier, Russian banker, mob associate, SOPRANOV hired KENT MANTRIBE in 2005 to run data mining and influence campaign in U.S. and in European democracies.

* WOODY and his inner circle have accepted a regular flow of intelligence from the Kremlin, including on his political rivals, specifically President Obama and Secretary Clanton.

* February, 2012, MANTRIBE in Moscow; SOPRANOV and MANTRIBE brief a cyber team, other oligarchs, and President TUTIN. French agent heard them talking about efforts to effect 2016 U.S. election.

* March 10, 2013, MANTRIBE, DASH ROCK, and U.S. resident ALEX SPLATER (Russian-born New York investor, Russian mob connections) meet SOPRANOV, TUTIN, and several other Russians and oligarchs. (Photos available.) Following that meeting, Russia moved over 5,000 new spy cadets to Moscow academy; mission/deployment unclear.

RUSSIAN INTELLIGENCE COMPROMISED WOODY DURING HIS MOSCOW VISITS TO BLACKMAIL HIM OVER MONEY AND SEX.

* November 10, 2013, WOODY met with SOPRANOV, TUTIN, and several other Russians and oligarchs. French and Dutch agents hear from sources in the room that SOPRANOV offered WOODY $50 million to seek

Republican nomination. SOPRANOV offer includes financing for hotel in Moscow AND investors for cable channel after presidential race. (Photo available)

* WOODY unknowingly hired U.S. agent as security for Moscow beauty pageant. She found Russian cameras and microphones in the suite where she delivered WOODY. She replaced the Russian cameras, which show multiple sex acts with Russian spies posing as prostitutes. (Extracted stills from hotel available.)

WOODY CAMPAIGN WORKING WITH RUSSIA TARGETING POLITICAL OPPONENTS IN AN HISTORIC PROPAGANDA CAMPAIGN.

* May 18, 2014 MANTRIBE meets Russian NIKOLAY ORLOV (leads TUTIN's cyberhacking unit) in Prague to lay out the scope, intentions and details of a propaganda campaign that was then already well underway, and still continues. (Extensive photos, sound available of meetings.) This is Russia's most visible battle in war against global democracy.

* Autumn, 2014, Russia aimed the cyber weapon at Congress, probing, to see what links Congressional staff would open. Unclear outcome of this operation. (Revealed to "Big Eight" at the time.)

OCTOBER 2015, U.S. VOTER ROLLS SCANNED, PROBED FROM A SERVER IN RUSSIA.

* It took U.S. law enforcement/CIA four months to ascertain who hacked them. Russia's MO: avoid credit.

* Unclear what, if anything, Russia got or learned from the probe.

* Russia has, during last three years, sprouted hundreds of troll farms – spies conducing campaigns intended to sway the 2016 elections in U.K., U.S., and coming European

elections in 2017, and beyond. The real people behind this global manipulation number in the tens of thousands, all safely behind computer screens in Russia.

RUSSIAN DIPLOMAT, MIKHAIL KULAGIN, WAS WITHDRAWN FROM WASHINGTON AT SHORT NOTICE.

* Russian source told French Moscow spy that TUTIN feared diplomat's involvement in U.S. presidential election operation would be exposed in U.S. media.

* Unclear what diplomat's involvement is, but such sudden removal is uncommon.

SNOWDEN ON CYBERATTACK TEAMS; GAVE RUSSIANS STOLEN INTELLIGENCE.

* U.S. agent retrieved two Booz Allen drives from Russia's Spy Academy – and got them to FBI – before Russians killed her.

* Western agent based in Moscow saw SNOWDEN multiple times arriving or leaving the office he shares with ORLOV at cyberhacking office. (Photos available)

TWO RUSSIAN MILITARY INTELLIGENCE OFFICERS SAY RUSSIA MAY INTERFERE WITH THE U.S. VOTE IN 2016.

* French spy on routine wiretap of Russian spies talking (English transcript of recording available)

CONGRESS LOOKS AWAY

Every single face in the room was pale and drawn. The dossier had the desired effect. The knowledge of what was going on scared the shit out of all of them.

"I know this is quite a lot-" Zack began.

"This Brit," the House Intelligence Committee Chairman interrupted him. "Who the hell is he and why do we put more stock in what he says than what our own intelligence is saying."

"Mr. Chairman," Jules purred. "I'm the CIA asset on this task force – and this dossier is very much a product of NATO spies in Moscow. CIA is a contributor to this."

"But it is not an FBI-generated document," the House Speaker verified.

"Correct," Jules answered. "It was generated by a private contractor, in conjunction with several sources from several nations. Do you want to see the supplemental documents?"

Nobody said a word.

"I would," said the top Democrat on the Senate Intelligence Committee.

Jules laid out the photos on the table in front of the task force team. Nobody wanted to be the first to broach them.

The senator who'd asked to see them finally got up and approached them gingerly. "What am I looking at?"

Pointing, Jules said, "This is from late 2012, early 2013, late 2013. These are reports and literal transcripts, although we've all gotten better at blocking surveillance."

"All these things are going on in Russia. What U.S. laws were broken?" asked the top Democrat on the House Intelligence Committee.

"Odd as it sounds, none of this violates U.S. law," Zack said. "There is a separate investigation into money laundering."

He glanced at Max.

"One of the things brought to us by the CIA was stolen banking information which we could not use in a prosecution, but which we can share with you to help you judge our efforts."

"What is the other investigation?" asked one of the Republicans.

"I don't want to specify targets, but most or all of the targets noted in the dossier are getting a good look," Zack said slowly and deliberately. "All are related to Russian money laundered to Americans involved in this."

"Oh my god," mumbled the Republican Chairman of the House Intelligence Committee, a former D.A.

* * * *

The members of Congress facing their briefers were mortified, albeit for different reasons. Even these seasoned pros could not completely hide their revulsion.

"This is a war of manipulation," Danny began. "As we tweet, react, and vote on social media, Americans generate a treasure chest of data on what we think, how we respond to ideas and arguments, every second."

"These digitized convictions are available to anyone with money and computing power. Algorithms divide us into thousands of subgroups by region, religion, education, politics, and entertainment preferences."

"Moscow's trolls have perfected algorithms that we created here, delivered to Moscow by Snowden, to find hot-button issues and who is most susceptible. They craft messages to influence us, deploying either humans or automated computer programs known as 'bots,' to try to alter our voting behavior."

"They cannot change our behavior," huffed the Democratic Leader in the Senate.

"They already have, Sir," Danny said gently. "When we've found Russian bots, we've followed. We just watched a Russian bot in Ukraine infiltrate a U.S. social media group as a 42-year-old American housewife. The bot changed the political outlook of three in those chats."

"We've watched Russia make fake Facebook accounts appearing to be foreign media to send targeted reporters stories on political issues like refugees, the wall, NATO, realignment with Russia," Zack picked up on the briefing.

"They monitored who was susceptible to influence, and kept targeting private accounts of reporters they'd manipulated."

"In August, that idiot pharmaceutical chief declared that Hailey Clanton had Parkinson's," Danny picked up.

"Russian bots moved that everywhere, made it go viral. Same bots made it viral again after the Secretary fainted from dehydration yesterday."

Danny took off his glasses and rubbed his hand over his face in frustration and anxiety. "They already have changed our behavior," he finally intoned again. "A giant piece of the population believes complete bullshit!"

"Hey-" interrupted the House Speaker.

"They invented stories saying Pope Francis had endorsed Woody – or Secretary Clanton had murdered a DNC staffer," Max jumped in. "Just keeps getting more insidious."

"We just saw them make viral a story that Clanton ran a pedophile ring in a D.C. pizza parlor," Jules finished.

"Important context here: while it does appear they are changing behavior, it is from Russia, weaponized at select places in the U.S., and deals with a political campaign," Zack said, almost defeated. "It is insidious at a historic level. But it is not illegal for Russians to do that."

"Or to succeed at that," Jules interjected.

"It's not just on the right, it is on the far left too," Danny continued. "They are responding to similar ideas – empathy for Russia, desire to be economic partners, apathy for NATO, and weakness/sickness of Secretary Clanton – all themes circulating on both fringes."

Left out of the briefing was that the FBI was now probing how alt-right sites like Breitbart News and Infowars coordinated with Russian botnets to blitz social media with anti-Clanton stories, mixing fact and fiction when Woody did poorly in the campaign, earlier in the 2016 primaries.

* * * *

"This is a four step dance," Danny said, holding up a single finger. "Hackers steal damaging emails from their target – today, Democrats in the U.S."

Danny held up two fingers.

"They strategically inject a head fake – like in the middle of an unrelated message, they selectively edit the email with a sentence saying Mrs. Clanton made a deal with Wall Street Bankers to be their guy."

Danny held up three fingers.

"They dump the mass of emails out through Wikileaks."

Danny held up four fingers.

"Stories based on this edited information are posted on Twitter and Facebook by thousands of automated bots, then on Russia's English-language outlets, RT and Sputnik, then our own alt-right news sites such as Infowars and Breitbart – then Fox, and finally traditional journalists."

"*If* they ever get corrected, it's days later and the story's already dug in," Danny said, frustration barely visible, but boiling underneath.

"Russia was given voter rolls in multiple states, which the bots use to micro-target constituencies with the silver bullet of tailored political advertising for each voter," Jules dropped a little information pointing to a collusion of the Woody campaign and the Russian manipulators.

An uncomfortable silence fell over the Members of Congress.

"Who gave 'em voter rolls?" the Speaker asked quietly.

"We've narrowed it down to two suspects," Zack said.

"Was it a campaign?" another Republican asked.

"Yes."

Horror struck the faces of several, as it dawned on a couple of them: the Woody campaign had indeed actively colluded with the Russians.

"Help me understand it, how it is different than political advertising or PR that we already do," said the Senate Intelligence Chairman. "Use small words, please."

* * * *

"If you want white women in Pennsylvania to not vote, or Michigan independents to vote for minor parties – find out what they respond to, flood them with it."

"Russians and an American," – Danny deliberately left out names, although if they so much as glanced at the supporting evidence they were everywhere – "Set a theme … like Russia is a peace-loving country beat up on by NATO … or the Democrat is 'weak.' All the stories and posts will be a version of that to convince, say the young and unemployed, with whatever ideas or people they are already influenced by."

"Many on the left are being manipulated like this: Ms. Clanton will face a hostile Congress – nothing will get done – best to 'blow up the system' and start again by electing Woody."

"But they are targeting all demographics, across the political spectrum," said Zack.

"Yes," Jules said. "They're targeting evangelicals to ignore or forgive Woody's immorality – to get a Supreme Court justice to vote against gay marriage, abortion and elevate even hateful Christianity above all other faiths."

"Best part, once humans are fooled, they are loath to ever admit it," Danny said. "Humans would rather stay fooled – in the face of overwhelming evidence to the contrary. The blow to our id and egos would be debilitating."

* * * *

"Russian trolls rolled out a Twitter campaign at the end of August questioning the fairness of a Clanton victory," Zack said. "Days later, a new Russian PAC ran cable ads all over the country with the same message."

"They've consistently cast Woody as the target of unfair coverage from media outlets that vet information, do research, and employ reason," said Danny.

"You do know you are dissing a whole half of the population, there," said the Chairman of the Senate Intelligence Committee, indignantly.

"Your numbers are off, Mr. Chairman, but I am not dissing anybody," said Danny. "I'm worried for my fellow Americans who are being manipulated, with no warning from us whatsoever."

The four Republicans at the briefing were making eye contact – they were ready to leave. Woody was not under investigation, it seemed. That $50 million could have been a joke, or a spurned offer.

The Woody staffers mentioned in the British dossier were no longer with the campaign, so Woody had distance from any jeopardy they may be in.

They'd all concluded that – if the FBI task force was here briefing them on these matters – they didn't have what they needed for warrants, indictments ... all components of legal activity.

This was political. The FBI should get out of it.

The Democrats, however, were emboldened. They knew as long as they stayed and questioned, the FBI would stay. Already this one hour meeting was nearing two and a half hours.

* * * *

"Is Marc Glenn of interest to your investigation?" asked the top Democrat on the Senate Intelligence Committee.

Zack demurred, answering slowly to tell them more than he was saying. "He's not a target of an FBI investigation."

The California senator got it. "Is Glenn being investigated by anybody?"

Zack pursed his lips and blew out his breath. "He is, I believe, being investigated by the IG at DOD."

The senator nodded. She wasn't done. "Have you

followed money mentioned here?"

"We have," Zack said. "It's complex and two-tiered. There's what we have authority over, and what we do not. Max is a banker and, with the CIA, stole information to inform us how Russia is paying for things. Max?"

* * * *

The House Democratic Leader, who'd served on intelligence for decades asked, "Do you have a theory why the influx of so many spies?"

"Only theory," Jules said carefully, looking at Zack.

"So?" The House Democratic leader smiled. "If you knew, it'd be in this dossier. Your theory," she instructed.

"They've been sent here to pose as voters, to cast seemingly legitimate ballots, maybe under several disguises and IDs," Jules said. "That could make it close – or make the difference – in some of the swing states."

"Oh, that's bullshit," said the Senate Majority leader.

"We're convinced the hacking of voter databases was for a deeper reach into voting itself," Zack said, eyeballing the Leader. "But there is no evidence we have found that could convince a grand jury."

"As always, it could be a head fake," Jules said earnestly. "But indications are coming from our most reliable sources and assets in Moscow on this, from multiple, unrelated levels."

The silence was filled with many smart people sifting all this bad news through multiple filters.

Finally the Senate Majority Leader spoke, "So going public with all this puts the public stink of an FBI investigation on Woody – who so far as I can tell is *not* under investigation. Is that right?"

"He," Zack began slowly, so he'd be careful, and so

everybody else would know he was being careful for a reason.

"He is not presently under investigation in this counterintelligence operation," Zack finished slowly. He was, Zack left unsaid, considered a conspirator in terms of taking money to commit a fraud, under RICO statutes.

* * * *

Nearly four hours after the briefing began, the members of Congress were either: reeling from the crush of profound news, desperately trying to end the briefing, or just really needing to pee.

"Are we done now?" asked the House Speaker, about the fifth time one of the Republicans in the room had asked that.

"Being done indicates finality," intoned the top House Democrat on Intelligence. "There is no finality here. whenever this particular meeting ends, this is an ongoing matter."

"Yes," said Jules, grateful somebody appreciated that.

"I'm willing to suspend talking about this for right now, but I want contact information from each of you and your promise to answer our follow up questions," said the top Democrat on Senate Intelligence.

"Hey, voters need to know this, " said the top Democrat on House Intelligence.

"Doesn't warning the public help Russia damage confidence in the system?" asked the Republican Chairman of Senate Intelligence.

Zack shrugged. "There are two schools of thought on that."

The thin-lipped Senate Majority Leader spoke up again angrily.

"Listen here," he pointed at the briefers. "I flat don't believe the underlying intelligence the White House is shoving down our throats. He's trying to make this a campaign issue, and I won't let that stand."

"So you won't be part of a bipartisan statement condemning Moscow for this?" Jules asked, exasperated.

"Correct."

Eyes rolled around the room.

September 19, 2016

Tutin's boots migrated to Wisconsin for early voting to begin their general election mayhem. Well over half of all votes would be cast before Election Day, November 8.

September, 22, 2016

The senior Democrats on the Senate and House intelligence committees, issued a joint statement accusing Russia of underhanded meddling.

"Based on briefings, we conclude that the Russian intelligence agencies are making a serious and concerted effort to influence the U.S. election," they said.

September 26, Capitol Hill

Draped over each other, Zack and Jules slept in their bed. Zack's phone screeched.

They both stirred; Zack rolled over, picked up the phone, wiped his eyes, and read the message.

"DHS scanned most voting systems remotely across the country. Found and patched weaknesses. Some states also letting cybersecurity teams that check on site."

"I'll take any good news," Jules said, shaking herself

awake. "Taking the first shower?"

Sept. 28, 2016, Washington, D.C., House Judiciary Hearing

"Thank you, Director Commings," said the committee chairman. "The gentlewoman from Maryland."

The Director sipped water as he listened to the question. He half-expected it.

"Director, we are intimately familiar with the FBI investigation of the Clanton email server, in which you found no evidence of law breaking," she said. "Can you tell me if the Bureau is investigating connections between members of the Woody campaign and Russia?

"We do not confirm or deny investigations," Commings said.

She rolled her eyes, incredulously. "Really?"

* * * *

That afternoon, FBI Director Commings personally called the Florida Secretary of State to tell him there had been multiple attempts to intrude upon the voter registration systems.

The Oval Office

The 'Four Eyes' plus several other intelligence and law enforcement types gathered to decide how to tell the voters the Russians were up to something devious.

"Why the hell is NSA not convinced by this?" the President demanded of his Director of the National Security Agency, the holder of the nation's cyber weapons.

"The most critical Russian intelligence came from

France," the NSA Director said. "But we now view it with high confidence."

"That means now all U.S. spy agencies agree that Tutin directed this entire operation," the Director of National Intelligence said.

"Prepare a statement summarizing the intelligence in broad strokes," the president directed.

October 2, 2016; FBI's Russia Election Task Force

"There are some odd social media trends in Michigan, Wisconsin and Pennsylvania." Danny rubbed his eyes.

"Applying our algorithm, we saw key swing voters drawn to fake news and anti-Clanton stories."

"Google searches for the fake pedophilia story are disproportionately higher in swing districts, but not red districts."

"What are you saying? The manipulation is working?" Zack asked.

"YES!" Danny yelled, pushing back and standing up to pace. "YES! Why is that so fucking hard for everybody to believe? Can't convince Congress. Hell, we don't even believe it ourselves."

"The Russians may have altered behavior in key voting districts in key states," Danny slumped against the wall. "They've been at war with us for a couple of years now and we are just catching up."

"But how much?" asked Max. "Enough to swing the election?

"Surely no," Danny shrugged hopefully. "Voters can be smart."

"Have you met all the voters?" Max asked.

"Be nice. I'm an immigrant," Danny smiled. "I have faith in voters, in democracy."

"Isn't this what campaigns do, what advocates do all the time?" Jules asked. "Run ads, change voter's minds about issues and candidates? Companies do the same thing for products."

"Yes," Danny answered. "*American* campaigns. *American* advocates, even if they are bad actors. We've never had an adversarial state insert themselves into our elections, making this one deeply UN-democratic."

"So, *not* what campaigns and advocates do all the time," Zack nodded.

Jules looked at her phone, alarmed. She stood up.

"What?" Zack asked.

"Pierre's running. Needs us."

Zack stood up. Jules shook her head at him, her eyes narrow. "I'll take Max and use CIA air."

Zack looked unhappy, but resigned. He nodded, jaw clenched.

October 3, 2016; Puskin, Russia (south of St. Petersburg)

The U.S. Defense Attaché from Embassy Moscow got out of his car at the small house. Looking around, he didn't see anyone.

He knocked on the door, and was let in. Eyes adjusting to the dark, he looked for Pierre.

"Here," said the old woman, pointing at the bed.

"Dude, how bad is it," the Attaché asked, going to Pierre's side.

"Got me under the bottom of my vest, he said, looking pale. "I got to get out."

"We going to your zodiac in the Gulf?"

"Yeah."

* * * *

Speeding to the Gulf of Finland, Pierre noticed a helicopter overhead.

"Shit," he muttered.

"Diplomatic immunity," said the Attaché.

"Not from bullets," Pierre said.

* * * *

As they neared the Gulf, the helicopter got closer.

Pierre pulled out his gun, taking off the safety.

"Hang on," the Attaché said anxiously. He picked up a microphone and flipped a switch.

"This is a United States vehicle carrying two U.S. diplomats," he said with authority over a speaker. "We demand diplomatic immunity."

Then he picked up a phone from the car console.

"We're a couple of clicks from the gulf, being harassed by a chopper. Seeing it on drone? Can you call? Thanks."

The helicopter came so close over the car, it seemed like it would land on the roof, the shadow of it all around the car.

Pierre reached to lower the window.

"No kidding. Don't show the gun or they'll blow us away."

"They're gonna do that anyway."

"Hang the fuck on," the Attaché said forcefully. "The world's watching."

Suddenly, the helicopter pulled up and flew away.

* * * *

On the dirt road, the gulf suddenly appeared in front of them.

"It's on the right, other side of that rock," Pierre

pointed.

Car stopped, the Attaché said, "Hang here." He opened the bag, and inflated the zodiac.

He went back to the car, helped Pierre out, pulling his arm across his shoulder, and they walked back to the inflatable boat.

Dragging it to the edge of the water, he helped Pierre into it. "Not sure you can do this alone, buddy. I'm coming too."

He turned and autolocked the car, and pushed them into the gulf. He lowered the motor in the water and they moved quickly, jumping breaking waves.

* * * *

The sun was setting fast. Pierre saw a small sea plane descending toward them. He blew out his breath in relief.

The plane made a water landing and motored over to the zodiac.

Jules popped open the airlock and door, stepping down the ladder to stand on the pontoon.

"Hey, love," she reached for Pierre, who smiled weakly, for the first time. She helped him to the ladder, and Max held out his arms to grab Pierre and pull him up.

Jules shook hands with the Attaché. "Coming with, or heading back?"

"Back to the salt mines," he said affectionately. "Great to see you again Jules. Get him to a doctor."

"Roger that; remember I'm dead, don't tell anybody you saw me," she winked.

* * * *

The small plane took off.

October 4, 2016

Guccifer 2.0, a Russian cyber team, posted documents hacked from the Clanton Foundation, selectively edited.

Russian attacks – which had ceased for a few weeks – resumed. Russian military intelligence launched an operation against a software company, which provided voting software and devices to at least eight states.

GENERAL ELECTION

October 5, 2016; FBI's Russia Election Task Force

Jules and Max walked in, looking exhausted.

"Where're we at?" she asked Zack.

"The president and IC have decided to put out a statement on Russian hacking," he said softly, pointing at a page on the table.

"Pierre?" Zack asked in Jules' ear, hand on her back.

"We left him on a French hospital ship in the Gulf," she reported. "He was shot. I left two agents with him and they're headed to England. Champ'll bring him here."

Max was reading the short statement the task force was asked to weigh in on. "This is it?"

Jules grabbed it, read the long sentence, and looked at Zack quizzically.

He clenched his jaw, closed his eyes, shaking his head.

7:05 p.m.

Jules caught her breath.

Zack didn't hear it, but saw Max look at her with concern. She got up and went to the bathroom, where she sat down and began to cry.

Zack walked in.

Embarrassed, she wiped her face, stood and walked to the sink.

"It's the *ladies* room."

"Well, I'm just here for some girl talk," he said gently pulling her to his chest.

Losing all pretext of being a tough guy, Jules devolved into sobs, arms around Zack.

"It's OK, babe," he whispered quietly, rocking her. "It's OK. You need to sleep."

"IT'S NOT OK!" she gasped, holding on tighter. "We are failing. Russians are fixing our election. NOBODY CAN KNOW. We are completely fucked."

He rocked her as he said, "Not completely. Secretary Clanton will get elected. Congress will remain fucked up, but the Supreme Court will get back to the ideological balance of the 1970s."

He lifted her face. "Hey, you gotta have a little faith."

She pressed him in a hug. "I have faith in you. Of all the guys I ever – you know – you are the only one I ever trusted."

He knew what she meant. Jules didn't completely trust anybody. "I trust you, too, Jules," he whispered in her ear.

Eyes wet, she pushed back, touched his face and walked to the sink to wash her face and blow her nose.

He folded his arms and leaned against the next sink.

"I'm always your best friend," he said quietly. "I know trust is as far as you can go. I just …"

She reached for his hand. "Let's go home."

* * * *

Several hours later in their Capitol Hill house, Jules woke up with a start, her arm over Zack.

She rolled over on her back, arm on her forehead. Back to being perplexed. She narrowed her eyes and looked at Zack.

She cuddled up against his side, rubbing his chest.

"You awake?"

He grunted and turned over, still asleep.

Running her hand down his butt, she began to stroke him. That woke him up.

She climbed on top of him, straddling his face and they indulged in some acrobatic oral sex.

Breathing hard afterwards, he pulled her up to his chest.

"How'd that statement come to be?" she asked.

"It was all the unified intel and cops could agree on to say. President's trying hard not to politicize it, play into Tutin's hands."

"Isn't he doing that anyway?" she asked. "Letting politics shape our response to a national security threat?"

"Sometimes it feels like we're one of the groups helping Russia's campaign," Zack conceded.

"So there's us," Jules said, rubbing his chest. "Republicans who won't confront Moscow for a long shot at a Supreme Court justice. The media running email stories, as if Russia didn't edit them in advance."

"Democrats who've failed to tell the nation why we should give a shit that Russia is meddling in our affairs," Zack interjected.

"Like it'll matter if Russia wins," Jules said stoically. "Courts won't matter. Free press won't exist. And we certainly won't be in charge of our affairs anymore."

October 7, 2016, 3:30 p.m.

CNN's anchor followed the breaking news splash reading, "*In a joint statement, the Department of Homeland Security and the Director of National Intelligence said, 'The US Intelligence Community is confident that the Russian Government directed the recent compromises of emails from U.S. persons and institutions … and that Russia's senior-most officials authorized these activities.'"*

4:00 p.m

In the Russia-Election Task force, somebody stood and turned up the TV, saying, "Hey, listen to this."

An *Access Hollywood* tape revealed Woody talking badly about women.

Mouths around the room gaped open when he said, "Grab 'em by the pussy."

Jules nodded, "I know just how that goes with him."

4:30 p.m.

"Oh my God, Russia didn't let any time pass to absorb the pussy grabbing story," said Zack, looking at the tablet in front of him, then to his watch.

"Tape went public 30 minutes ago, and WikiLeaks is publishing stolen emails from Clanton's campaign chairman."

"Well, that's just GREAT," said Jules in frustration, throwing her hands in the air. "The country is never gonna hear about Russia. We can't possibly keep up."

October 12, 2016; FBI's Russia-Elections Task Force

Jules looked up as the CNN breaking news logo came up.

"Federal investigators believe Russian hackers were behind cyberattacks on a contractor for Florida's election system that may have exposed the personal data of Florida voters, according to US officials briefed on the probe.

"The hack of the Florida contractor comes on the heels of hacks

in Illinois, in which personal data of tens of thousands of voters may have been stolen, and one in Arizona."

October 14, 2016

Tutin's insurrection force went to Pennsylvania to apply for mail-in ballots.

Washington, D.C., FBI's Russia-Elections Task Force

"That's what we know so far," Zack said to the room, now bulging with agents from the NSA, State department and Defense department.

"We are seeking ideas for retaliation. Let's hear it," Jules added.

They started off ambitious.

"What's the downside of sector-wide economic sanctions – banks, oil, energy technology, trade, travel, U.N. resolutions … Congressional resolutions, stuff like that?" asked an official in a military uniform.

"Pare that back to sector wide sanctions – U.N. *can't* act – Russia will veto," Jules said. "Congress *won't* act. Bear in mind, Russia's success here indirectly rewards the majority in Congress."

"What about cyberattacks to take Russian networks offline?" asked as NSA official.

"We might as well shake a fist real good at them," said a naval officer. "We could move a carrier group into the Baltic Sea."

Those in this room did not know President Obama had already all but ruled out any pre-election retaliation against Moscow.

"Here's what the food chain above us fears," Jules offered. "Any action will be seen as political, and that

Tutin, motivated by a seething resentment of Clanton, is prepared to go beyond fake news and email dumps."

"We've got Russian attempts to penetrate election systems in 39 states so far, we've got to assume they'll get all 50," said a state department official. "Why are we not warning state election officials?"

"We have," Zack said, jaw clenched. "States run by Republicans don't want it."

* * * *

"The patchwork nature of our voting jurisdictions makes it hard for Russia to swing the outcome, but it could sow chaos during the election and beyond," said a cyber geek.

"It is also likely that Russia will fabricate more explosive material," Zack added.

"Politics ain't my corner of the jungle," said an army officer, "But isn't Secretary Clanton going to win?"

That certainty contributed to the lack of urgency outside the task force.

Jules put her head in her hands. Danny was right. Nobody believed this could really happen.

Not this room.

Not Congress.

Not the Administration, which settled on a series of warnings, in an effort *not* to help Tutin's effort.

"It's a good idea to war game out scenarios that can pop on Election Day," said one of the suits.

"Great minds," said Zack. "The President asked us to throw them the most likely scenarios, which they will wargame the week before the election."

* * * *

The Task Force threw out a big net in a series of bulletins suspicious of Russian nationals, with particular interest in violent deaths of white men between 20-40 in the northeast, or along the eastern corridor.

The bulletins went to field offices, hospitals, morgues, and law enforcement jurisdictions in the targeted area.

October 15, 2016; The White House, Oval Office

While "red phones" in the White House and Kremlin once protected the world from nuclear annihilation, today's red phone transmitted messages and documents over fiber-optic lines to defuse a possible cyber conflict.

The DNI laid a page on the President's desk. "Here's the message. And we transmit all these documents."

The CIA had scrubbed the documents for days.

The president read it aloud. "Attached are documents that support the following conclusions.
1. Russian military intelligence hackers are trying to take over the computers of 122 local election officials.
2. Russian hackers hit election systems in at least 39 states.
3. Russian troll farms continue to direct a massive influence campaign against American voters.
4. Russian spies were dispatched to cast ballots in the election. We continue to round them up."

The president paused. "So, that's the head fake." He shot a look at the ceiling, then began again.

"5. We are certain this effort is directed by Russian leaders, solely to elect one candidate and defeat the other.

This invasion is dangerously aggressive.

I warn your nation that these attacks risk a far broader conflict.

Continued work by Russia on these fronts will continue to be considered a military attack on the United States homeland.

Please cease all these activities."

He looked around the Oval Office he would leave in three months. "Any dissent?"

His advisors shook their heads. No dissent.

"Send it," he ordered.

The DNI opened the laptop and hit a series of keys. "Done." It was 8:30 a.m.

"How long you think they take to respond?"

"What if they don't."

"Don't know, and one bridge at a time," the President said.

Moscow, Russia; The Kremlin, Tutin's office

As the U.S. election day grew closer, Orlov, Sopranov, and Tutin gathered at the end of each day for vodka and gossip from their U.S. spies.

The loud ping from the office startled all three men.

"Fire alarm?" asked Sopranov.

"Mr. President," his military assistant called urgently. "The red phone! The Americans are sending a message."

All three ran to Tutin's desk, reading it together.

Eyes continuing to run through it, Orlov said, "He's lying. We do daily head counts of the boots."

"But he knows," Tutin said.

"He don't know shit. Fuck him," said Sopranov.

Tutin sat back, looking thoughtful. The old KGB warhorse was working through his options.

October 16, 2016; The White House, Oval Office

The next day Tutin responded. "This matter concerns me greatly. It is untrue. Please provide more evidence. You have my assurance that we will look into the substance of your information."

The president looked at the DNI.

"They're ignoring us. They think they've got us."

"Is it possible the 2012 election was the last free election America will see?" the DNI asked quietly.

The president's eyes wet, he patted the DNI's shoulder. "Let's pray that's not the case."

October 17, 2016

Tutin's insurrection force moved to Michigan to apply for mail-in ballots.

Washington, D.C., Capitol Hill

The population in the Capitol Hill house Zack and Jules shared with Max increased by two.

The band was back together.

Champion, using a cane and still walking with a limp, handed Pierre a Gatorade. Pierre was weak and pale.

* * * *

"Are you still confident Secretary Clanton will win?" Pierre asked Zack over dinner and after the obligatory cross examination about his health.

"Oh yeah," Zack said.

"After Brexit? And so many of my own countrymen fessing up that they had no fucking idea what they were doing?" Champion retorted.

"Yeah, I'm not so sure about 'confident,'" Jules said, swirling her wine. "It is much closer than the pollsters think it's gonna be. She's gotta win by way more than 100,000 votes in states Democrats usually win."

"This is where the influence campaign is focused?" Pierre asked.

"Yeah, in those states," Max said, stretching. "It's just – with all I know, the pollsters' math is flawed."

"Feeling a tad better," Jules said, pulling out a 15-page document, and handing it to Champion for him and Pierre to eyeball.

"It's the White House plan to deal with an Election Day attack," she said. "We can't stop a final Russian attack on the vote. Since states are the arbitrator of elections, in most cases, we'll defer to them on hacking."

"If they stop the voting or blow up a polling place-"

"Attacks with noise and smoke," Pierre huffed.

"Right," she nodded at him. "We deploy FBI if they halt voting, and Guard or reserves if there's violence. There's even a task force for post-election stuff, like dealing with planted stories questioning the results."

Pierre set the document down, sat forward, elbows on the table, and looked hard at Jules and Zack.

"You *really* think Clanton will win?"

"Yes," said Zack. "But it'll be ugly."

Jules paused. "Yes, she wins. Will their boots in the four target states upset the Electoral College? That, I don't know."

October 26, 2016

As early voting began in Florida, Tutin's insurrection migrated back to Florida to cast 25 votes per boot by

October 28. It'd be a marathon two days.

Washington, D.C., FBI's Russia-Elections Task Force

In a letter to Congress, FBI Director Commings updated them on the Bureau's closed investigation into Hailey Clanton's private email server.

Jules picked up the letter with distaste. "So you tell Congress, and they tell the world we're looking at emails of a Clanton adviser whose dick of a husband is under FBI scrutiny?"

"I said it better in the letter," the Director shrugged his already sagging shoulders. He'd been through the ringer in the last 24 hours, running down all the angles.

"I'm only revealing it – at all – to protect Clanton's coming presidency from Congress investigating fake Russian documents. In a Clanton administration, we'll need Congress to trust us about what's fake."

October 28, 2016

Tutin's insurrection marched back to Pennsylvania to mark and mail 23 ballots. The next day, they drove to Michigan to mark and mail 25 ballots.

* * * *

The CIA Director watched the reporter walk in his office alone, as he'd requested.

Shaking hands, he gestured the reporter from one of the major news dailies to sit down.

"This is not in my nature," the CIA Director explained. "The FBI laid all this out for Congress in September and they were not moved to do shit.

Meanwhile, nearly half of Americans have voted while this … is unknown."

"Who wrote this?" the reporter asked. "I need to talk to the author and verify it."

"I certainly appreciate that, but that's a different standard from when your publication printed emails like they were written by Clanton's guys. After you knew they'd been edited by Russia."

The Director sighed.

"Hey, it's not like I'm your drunk uncle with a conspiracy theory. I don't know if I can hook you up with the author. I can show you supplemental materials here in my office, but you cannot mention them in your story."

Another five variations of that conversation with the national security correspondents of other major news organizations repeated themselves over the course of the day.

In the end, no news organization at all ran a story based on the explosive contents of the dossier.

The same people that gleefully ran Russian-edited emails from the Clanton campaign hesitated to report such salacious allegations, despite being attested to by the spy boss of the United States.

MOSCOW CLEANS UP

Oct. 31, 2016; Milwaukie, WI, Elections Supervisor's Office

"We have a significant increase in the number of absentee voters compared to the last general election," said the clerk to the supervisor behind the desk. "We might even have many more absentee votes than we have absentee voters."

The supervisor's jaw dropped.

"Somebody's stuffed the box?" the supervisor said.

"Truthfully, I don't know," the clerk shrugged. "Our voting systems are just old and susceptible to hackers."

November 1, 2016, The White House, Situation Room

President Obama walked in to join his National Security Council, "Begin the simulation."

His Chief of Staff began, "Voting is stopped at 20 precincts in Michigan."

For the next five hours, they war-gamed various Russian Election Day attacks, running through fictional events to rehearse how they would communicate and respond in a real attack.

Scenarios included actual vote meddling – voters being turned away from voting, or attacks at polling places – while others focused on responding, post-election, to efforts undermining the election result.

On the way out, the President mumbled to his chief, "That scared me more than I thought it would."

Nov. 5, 2016; Washington, DC, Russia Election Task Force

"Guess we should have expected this," Danny said. "Bot traffic just skyrocketed, today targeting left wing voters. Seems like all the messages are encouraging votes for the Green Party candidate."

Staring at the screen, he added, "Russians also urge voters to write in Banders' name, or to not vote at all, reminding them of the made up shit from the primaries."

Finger on the screen, Danny said, "Today's Russian theme for the left is 'voter fraud' by the DNC, skewing the vote for Hailey, blocking news coverage of Ernie."

November 7, 2016

Tutin's insurrection marched back to Pennsylvania for the last time, to cast their last two ballots per boot the following day.

They weren't alone. Felix Slater sent hundreds of East Coast wise guys – none Russian – to mess with polling places in Pennsylvania's six population centers to depress voting where Secretary Clanton was heavily favored.

Hundreds more wise guys were doing the same in Wisconsin, Michigan and Florida.

Moscow, Russia, Outside the U.S. Embassy

The American spy was running for his life. Chased by a Russian shooting at him, he was ducking and weaving.

One of the bullets hit him in the vest, knocking him down.

Struggling to get back up, he could see the U.S. Marine Embassy Guard headed toward him, gun drawn.

Just 10 yards further.

On his feet, the spy ran toward the Marine. Other Marine Guards appeared and fired back.

The spy put his arm over the Marine's shoulder in gratitude.

The spy's head exploded, spewing the area with blood and gray matter. Marines hustled inside with the body.

Washington, DC, FBI's Russia Election Task Force

"Holy shit," Jules said into the phone, alarmed. "Got security footage, right?"

"Goddamnit!" shouted Pierre, looking at his phone. "Everybody's embassy in Russia should destroy information and move people to the Swiss embassy."

Furiously punching his phone, he repeated that in French to the French ambassador in Moscow.

"What?" asked Zack, standing up, looking at his friends, all of whom looked pale and frantic.

Champion, looking at his phone, blanched, saying, "I just lost two sources, both killed in London."

Jules hung up. "The Russians are cleaning up. Moscow Station is missing three spies.

"Video here from Moscow Station," a geek called out.

"Throw it up please," Jules said.

While they watched the exchange of gunfire in front of the embassy, Jules bit her lip. "I recruited him for this station." They all groaned as his head exploded.

"Our defense attaché was found dead in his car last night," she continued.

"No," Pierre moaned, mourning the man who got him to Jules last month. "Call your station, love. Get them to the Swiss."

She called the CIA director urgently.

ELECTION DAY – November 8, 2016
5:30 a.m., White House, Eisenhower Office Building

Jules and Zack opened the door to "Sit Room Two," a second Situation Room across the street from the actual one in the White House. Geeks were already running a secure video conference with other agencies and nations.

The room was full. Once the polls opened, nobody would leave until results were announced.

Joined today by election-crimes coordinators from the Justice Department, and other western spy agencies, this would constitute the President's brain trust in any response situation today.

New York City, NY, Russian Consulate

An hour after the polls opened, police and emergency responders responded to a 911 call about an unconscious man inside the Russian consulate.

"This way," said a Russian guard as they arrived.

Hurrying inside, they found Sergei Krivov, 63, dead at the scene.

An EMT felt for a pulse and shook his head.

"What happened?" a cop asked.

"He fell from roof," lied one Russian official.

"No, heart attack," lied another.

Looking at the giant wound on Krivov's head, the cop said, "So he fell off the roof, knocked a hole in his head, then died of a heart attack?"

"O.K.," smiled the first Russian diplomatic liar.

Detroit, Michigan, Midday, Election Supervisor's office

"Shit, this is a bigger mess than usual," she said on the phone, just at the edge of frantic. "In Detroit, 59% of optical scanners simply 'broke' this morning. We don't have the manpower to manually count our ballots."

Jacksonville, Florida, Polling Place

Faces scrunched in confusion, election workers watched voting machines leave a paper trail showing a vote for Woody when the voter selected Clanton.

The election volunteer wearing a "Clanton Observer" button asked the election official, "May I photograph it?"

"No," the election official shook her head.

Punching the phone, the Clanton election observer walked toward the door to report in.

"I've seen a half dozen Clanton voters vote the right way, but the machine counts the result for him."

"We're getting hundreds of reports like this and we're looking at giant anomalies from early returns," the voice on the phone said. "Document it all."

Tampa, Florida, Polling Place

A long line of frustrated voters was reaching a breaking point.

"What's the hold up?" asked a voting official.

"We can't locate thousands of voters in our system," said the poll worker, phone to his ear. Suddenly he held up his finger.

"I'm in Tampa," he said. "The digital database is wrong. There is a lot of confusion."

Orlando, Florida, Polling Place

A line backed up in the polling place as voters stood there, holding ballots to feed into the digital scanner.

"Ladies and gentlemen, please be patient, we've had a dozen ballot scanners stop working today," one of the election officials explained.

In Apopka, outside of Orlando, two polling places ran out of ballots and began turning voters away.

Broward County, Florida, Polling Place

Late in the afternoon, an election official hung up the phone.

"Everybody listen up – we have a bomb threat," said the official. "Everybody needs to leave quickly, but please do not run."

She grabbed the arm of an older woman, "I'll help you out. Everyone remember, do not push."

The bomb threat shut down the largest Democratic precinct in the county for two hours, sending thousands of elderly voters home without casting a ballot.

Milwaukee, Wisconsin, Office of the Elections Supervisor

Late on Election night, the clerk came into the Supervisor's office.

The Supervisor sat with his hands on his head. "I'm fairly convinced the electronic voting machines around the state have been hacked. The numbers are wrong."

"I just did a quick analysis," the clerk said. "Across Wisconsin, Clanton got seven percent fewer votes in counties with electronic-voting machines, compared with counties that used optical scanners and paper ballots."

The supervisor, hands on his face in horror, stared. "That's nowhere near an anomaly. I need a lawyer."

The clerk tapped the papers in her hand.

"Based on my stats, Clanton may have been denied as many as 30,000 votes," the clerk gave the bottom line. "We're done counting, she lost Wisconsin by 27,000."

The supervisor reached for a phone.

* * * *

When Wisconsin's vote margin was finally announced, Woody's winning margin was 0.7%

As one side of the political divide erupted in full-throated victory, the majority of American voters watched in shocked surprise ... and raw fear.

Disbelief turned to stunned despair and tears.

Woody was winning several Democratic-leaning states, against all odds. He won Pennsylvania by 1.2%, Florida by 1%, and Michigan 0.3%.

The nation, and the world, were astonished. Afraid.

2:00 a.m., Eisenhower Office Building

The twenty-ish people still in "Sit Room Two" sat dumbfounded, staring at TV screens all telling them the same thing.

Most were standing, hands on their heads, over their mouths – generally in horror.

Jules sucked in her breath, holding back tears.

"The Russians won," she said loudly. She shook her head to clear it.

"Pierre," she said plainly shaken, but thinking. "Was this the last battle? Or are we midway through this?"

Eyes bleary, Pierre looked at Jules, lost. "Just too soon

to say, love. I don't know-" he choked out, then got up and walked to the wall, leaned against it and sobbed.

She caught eyes with the other original members of the team, and went to Pierre, pulling him into a hug – not romantic – the hug one warrior gives another after a lost battle.

They clung to each other; Pierre was inconsolable.

Zack, Max and Champion joined them, hands on their shoulders.

The Director, almost catatonic, finally spoke.

"Everybody go home. Sleep. Drink. Whatever," he said, his voice empty.

"Let's meet back here at noon. Try not to think about things until then. I'm attaching teams from the field office to watch your backs."

He rose, patting Danny on the shoulder, who was quietly wiping his red, wet eyes. His faith in democracy had taken quite the fall down the stairs.

Zack looked at his phone. "Did we know they killed Sergei Krivov in New York this morning?"

"Of course they did," said Max quietly.

"Felix's local Russian money contact," Jules nodded.

November 9, 2016

Tutin's insurrection force rose, shocked and amazed that they had pulled it off. Now all that was left was a deft disappearance.

Moscow, Russia, Russian Parliament

Tutin stepped up to the podium to make an unbelievable announcement.

"Good news," Tutin said. "Dale Woody has been

elected President of the United States!"

Russia's Parliament erupted in a long, loud, sustained standing ovation. Many in the parliament had an inkling of what Tutin and his government were doing to undermine the west.

This was a new day. Their day. Their old adversary was in the ditch, their government engine mostly dead.

FBI's Russia Election Task Force Office, noon

The TV screens were reporting on Hailey Clanton's concession and the protests that were breaking out on American streets.

"First, this task force remains – your job has never been more important," the Director began as he looked at the team. He bit his lip. "But let's not kid ourselves. These guys will try to end our work."

"So we are going to hide you," he said. "Soon as we can, we are relocating you to the CIA."

"You five," he pointed to Zack, Jules, Champion, Max and Pierre, "We want to relocate back to London first, mostly to reunite Champ with his family there, hide the rest of you outside the country, see where this goes."

The Director stood up to pace.

Zack suddenly said, "Boss, they are gonna fire you shortly after noon on January 20."

"That's … exactly how long we have," the Director said, dejectedly. "Champ, you should relocate your family right away. We may need to release the dossier."

Champion nodded, pulled out a blank pocket card and began making notes.

"For today, let's go around the room, see where we are, what we can shuffle-" he dry heaved, held up a finger, and took off for the bathroom.

"Not sure he deserves so much blame for this. GEEZ!" Jules said in frustration – easily the 20th time she'd done so in the last 12 hours.

November 25, 2016, The White House, Oval Office

President Obama sat at his desk, facing his advisors. Beside him a newspaper was headlined: *Possible Challenges to the Vote in Wisconsin, Pennsylvania and Michigan.*

"What the hell do we say about this? People's faith in the system is a fragile thing," he said, holding up the paper. "Once people lose faith that the elections are fair and honest, our entire system of government is in jeopardy."

"We passed the line of being in jeopardy two weeks ago, sir," said the CIA Director.

"Suppose we walk a fine line on a statement, futzing the free and fair part," said Director Commings. "Do we do democracy a favor fudging that this was a fair result? Knowing there were 400,000 votes from Russian spies? And more from malware?"

"Can you prove that?" the former law professor asked his FBI Director, knowing the answer.

"No sir," he answered quietly. "Not in court."

"We don't have it." He stared at his hands on the desk. "We have to stand behind the election results," he said slowly. "Recounts will proceed or not, but we need to formally support the Election Night result."

"Look, we tried to secure the vote, but got mired in partisan muck," he shook his head. "Laid awake most of the night. We're doing this because our vulnerability to election meddling is less about the last election, and more about the next one."

* * * *

Later that day, the White House released a statement saying, "We stand behind our election results, which accurately reflect the will of the American people and we believe our elections were free and fair from a cybersecurity perspective."

Adding the last four words kept the President from being a liar. From a cybersecurity perspective, the election ended better than anyone could have imagined. Except they could not prove the malware had moved ballots.

No mention of the boots. That would have validated and supported Tutin's goal.

November 29, 2016; Delaware River, on a boat headed east

Four young Russian spies, the last boots still in the U.S., were in a boat heading out of Philadelphia, ostensibly to hook up with a dozen of the other spies who had decided to jump ship and hide in the northwest of the U.S., or Canada, rather than return to Russia.

"Biggest challenge," one of the men said, "Will be evading our own people here."

The woman smiled, and poured vodka heavily laced with Fentanyl into shot glasses for her targets.

They toasted, "Na zdorovye!" and downed the shot glasses, slamming them down again. Immediately, the eyes of each man became heavy and blurred. They were too impaired to move.

"Your biggest challenge <u>was</u> to evade your own people here," she said in Russian, then shot each one in the head.

She cleaned off in the galley and changed clothes. Pulling up to a private dock, she jumped out, sank the boat and stole another one, taking off again.

November 30, 2016; FBI Russia Election Task Force

"Zack," a woman had opened the door to the room, and pointed at the phone in the center of the table.

"Philly PD, call came through the desk. About your bulletin on unidentified bodies violently killed."

"Tolliver," he said into the phone, listening for a moment. "Keep security on them; I'm sending agents."

The White House, National Security Council Room

"So we penetrate Russian networks with malware and just … let it lay?" the President quizzed his national security team.

"Right," the DNI said. "It's the cyber equivalent of laying bombs inside all their networks – under their feet – invisible and harmless until activated."

"You have reason to think Woody will screw his new patrons like that?" the President smiled sarcastically.

"Not really-" the CIA Director began.

"You still have two months to decide," Director Commings said. "And gives the nation a weapon to activate if things get nastier with Russia."

"The Treasury Department has robust sanctions, hitting entire sectors of their economy," the DNI said. "They did ask we subtract Kaspersky Lab-"

"Moscow's cybersecurity firm," Director Commings interjected.

"Thinking is Europe – and some U.S. companies – use Kaspersky systems and software," the DNI finished.

"Let's keep perfecting this," the President said. "I want to announce new sanctions before the new year."

December 1, 2016; New York, NY, Woody's Worldwide

Woody's grandson greeted Russia's U.S. ambassador at the Woody in-house transition office.

Gen. Marcus Glenn walked in before they sat down.

"Marc!"

"Mr. Ambassador, so good to see you again."

"Please sit," said Woody's grandson. "The new president asked me to talk to you about setting up a secret and secure communications channel between our transition team and the Kremlin."

"We are hoping to use Russian diplomatic facilities here to have candid pre-inaugural talks," Glenn said.

"That could be difficult," the ambassador hedged, knowing he wouldn't expose Russia's secret network.

December 5, 2016

Detroit News headline read: *"Half of Detroit votes may be ineligible for recount."*

"Widespread voting problems could mean more than 50% of Detroit precincts can't be recounted, directly calling into question whether Dale Woody won Michigan," the story read.

December 10, 2016; Moscow, Russian, Intelligence Office

Two Russian military officers entered the office with three of their colleagues: a Russian computer security expert and two high-level intelligence officers who worked on cyber operations.

Pulling weapons, one officer said, "You are under arrest, for treason." Pulling one of his colleagues' arms back and handcuffing him, he hissed, "You gave the Americans information."

Putting them in a truck in front of the building, they shot each in the back of the head and took off slowly.

SETTING THE STAGE

December 15, 2016; FBI, Director's Office

"That's where we're at on the money laundering," Max said. "What's up with the rest of it?"

"Obama's order to review Moscow's interference prompted analysts to go back through files, scouring for overlooked clues," the Director said.

"Their conclusions … well, our task force could have written that same report last August."

Max rolled his eyes.

December 19, 2016

Washington Post headline read, "*Electoral College: Woody, 304, Clanton, 227.*"

December 20, 2016; Ankara, Turkey

The Russian ambassador to Turkey, Andrey Karlov, was speaking at an art opening. "Art shows who we are."

The same Armenian assassin who'd shot Champion in the Caymans was dressed as a Turkish police officer.

The Armenian stepped in front of Karlov, shouted, "Do not forget Syria," and shot the ambassador at point-blank range. Syria, of course, was the head fake.

December 26, 2016; Moscow, Russia

One of the few remaining U.S. spies in Moscow was with a Marine in plain clothes.

They approached the car on the street, with a dead man inside, his head on the steering wheel.

"Who is it?" The Marine asked, inspecting the bullet holes in his head and back.

"Oleg Erovinkin," the spy said, shooting photos. "He was a source for Jules; he's in, was in, Russian intel."

Moscow, Russia, home of Petr Polshikov

Two hooded figures entered the suburban home of Petr Polshikov, 56, a senior Russian diplomat, just as his wife was pulling out of the driveway.

Polshikov had been one of Champion's sources. He'd called in sick today and had not left the house.

Creeping through the halls, they walked right into his bedroom, to the bed where he was sleeping, water and tissue paper sat beside a book.

One of the figures held a silenced weapon to his head and fired. Polshikov's eyes popped open in reflex, dead.

December 29, 2016, Kailua, Hawaii

President Obama, at a microphone, began quickly. "Today, we enact our first sanctions against Russia in retaliation for its interference in the 2016 election."

"We begin with the seizure of two Russian facilities and the expulsion of 35 suspected spies. We include sector-wide economic sanctions, including energy, defense, banking, travel, tourism. We urge other nations to sanction these sectors as well."

"There are other ways we are punishing the Russian leadership," he said. "Some of them will be seen and some will be unseen, allowing us to respond at a time of our own choosing, and for our own purposes."

Following the public announcement, Obama signed a secret order, authorizing a new covert program involving the NSA, CIA, FBI and U.S. Cyber Command.

It would be the new formal home to Zack and Jules' task force at CIA.

* * * *

Marc Glenn was busy that day in New York.

"Mr. Ambassador," he said in the phone. "Pass on our assurances that once Woody is inaugurated, sanctions will be lifted. The President-elect cannot say that publicly, but he has the sole power to overturn them."

It was the fifth time General Glenn spoke to the Russian ambassador that day, assuring their friends in Moscow that Woody was still solidly their guy.

Langley, Virginia, CIA, Task Force Red

In their new CIA digs, the FBI's Task Force on the Russia-2016 election was now nebulously named "Task Force Red."

"Possible they close us down, but keep this up as long as you can," said the CIA Director, seated beside Director Commings. He looked around at the room full of people, many of whom they'd scatter around the country and the world to make them harder to find.

"Max will keep working with Task Force Red from London, and also with the financial crimes unit at Treasury, where our money laundering charges will reside," Director Commings said.

"The only FBI investigation we leave open is the counter intelligence op looking at Woody, and the names listed in the dossier – which I have to brief him on next week," Commings shook his head and closed his eyes.

"January 19, we relocate our five guys" – now the shorthand for Jules, Zack, Champion, Pierre and Max – "to London," the CIA Director picked up. "Expect we'll move you again, before long. Jules, this is yours now."

"We got the Russian mob, Russian spies, Armenians – all aiming at us," Jules began.

"We got your back," the CIA Director said.

"Both of us," Director Commings said.

"Well, you're out in 20 days," said Jules pointing at her director. "And you," she pointed at Director Commings. "Same 20 days. Or however long it takes him to fire you."

She blew out her breath.

"We all know we are on the run," she said, spreading her hands on the table. "Woody and the Russians need to kill us, minimize evidence of their crimes."

"Going forward, 'Red' is about figuring ways we can undermine Russian manipulation efforts in real time," she finished. "I wanna hand them their ass back."

"Congress wants to kill science and technical creativity," Danny said. "I've started a nonprofit in Canada – Geeks United – of former U.S. military, NSA officers, and our own hackers. For ideas and context they don't have to conform to alternate facts."

"We've got two goals," Jules said. "Until we leave for London, we finish hiding our investigations in various agencies throughout the government."

"Also," she continued, "The three dead Russians in Philly were spies we ID-ed from photos Marines took off the body of my colleague the Russians murdered in front of Embassy Moscow."

She sucked in her breath. "That's what he died bringing home," she said quietly. "Identities of the 4,000 spies who voted here so many times."

"If Woody keeps doing his bluster-stumble routine after he's sworn in, it's possible we can keep doing work on criminal cases long before they find us," Zack added, giving her a minute to organize her thoughts.

"We've drafted the RICO charges for Mantribe, Rock, Splater and Woody for money laundering and fraud," he said. "DOD's Inspector General has always shared her Gen. Glenn case; she's ready to charge him for failing to register as a foreign agent and report Russian money."

"We will keep a careful log of all contacts between Woody and the Russians, past, present and future," Champion added. "Connect the assassinations. Leave a trail for governments to follow."

"The eye-on-the-ball aim here is to ensure they don't meddle in future American, European or other western elections – and to get, and stay, ahead on this front," Pierre finally joined in. "France has elections in a few months."

"In a few days, we release our joint report," Director Commings said.

"Congress isn't going to act," Max said angrily.

"They may eventually, but I don't see it," Zack said.

"We're ready to release the dossier," said Champion. "Each one of us are giving it to a different news guy."

January 6, 2017

Declaring the nation's election structures "vital to our national interests," the Homeland Security Secretary designated U.S. election systems as critical infrastructure, in order to make elections safer from tampering.

This time, he didn't give a damn how the Russians and the Alt-Right lied about it. Conservative states yawned. They'd won, fair and … well, their guy was president.

Woody would undo whatever Obama's guy was doing.

New York City, New York, Woody's Worldwide

Obama's Directors of the CIA, FBI and the National Director of Intelligence gathered to brief the incoming president.

Director Commings had the slimy job of pulling the president-elect aside and briefing him one-on-one about the details of the dossier, in the context of their united consensus that Russia interfered with the 2016 election.

The job for the other two was to brief Woody on the report being released that day.

Woody welcomed them into his office. "So, all done with the Russia crap?"

"Not exactly," said the CIA director, pulling out a slim book. "We are releasing a report on it today with unanimous findings from law enforcement. Do you … want to read through it or would you rather just hear what's in it?"

His jaw already angrily set, he said, "What's in it?"

* * * *

Everybody was up and tersely saying goodbye.

Director Commings was up. "Mr. President-elect, can I get you alone? It's a personally sensitive matter."

"Sure," Woody watched the door close as the CIA Director and DNI hurried out of the room.

"You asked a couple of times about the basis of the

report," Director Commings said, pulling out the single page, printed on both sides.

"This is a dossier compiled by several western intel agents – some of it we have been able to verify, some is spy-best-guessing."

Woody was pale. He was clearly stunned.

"Can't tell you how I hate to be the one to tell you about this, but it has been seen in the National Security Council and Congress," the Director said. "It is unfair that you be the only one *not* to have seen it."

Woody dropped the page on this desk, then pushed it out of his field of vision. "You can't prove any of that."

The Director saw Woody's usual bluster was gone.

"Hey, am I under investigation?"

He was talking to a rookie, nevertheless, the Director was careful. "Mr. President-elect, you are not the subject of an open counter-intelligence investigation."

The rookie did not know to inquire further.

"I want you to say that, then," Woody said unhappily.

"That … has other repercussions," the Director said. "Such as, if that were to change for some reason, it would legally require a public correction. Let's hold on to that."

Repugnant as this exercise was, the Director needed the president to get off his ass, but not hold him responsible for the investigation. Like that could happen.

* * * *

Jumping into the SUV outside, Director Commings said to Zack, "Get the whole conversation?"

"Yeah. He's so gonna fire you, Boss."

"Uh-huh," the director said absently, opening his laptop. "He's so gonna lie about my end of that. Writing a meeting memo for the file now."

"Hey, that's the way to claw him into the counter-intel investigation. He's gonna try to get you to close it down. Then he'll fire you. Obstruction. Trap they all fall into."

"So I'll leave a trail of paper laying out the story," the Director said, already writing the memo.

"Classified and unclassed," Zack suggested. "We're gonna need to find courageous reporters."

* * * *

The CIA, FBI and NSA released their unclassified report, concluding unanimously, "Vadik Tutin ordered an influence campaign in 2016 aimed at the U.S. presidential election."

The 17 U.S. national security agencies agreed that Tutin and "the Russian government aspired to help President-elect Woody's election chances when possible."

The report also – for the first time – drew a direct line between WikiLeaks and Russian military intelligence, causing consternation in actual journalistic circles.

Dear God, had they unwittingly played Tutin's game to fuck democracy by pretending the edited emails were news-worthy as presented on WikiLeaks' site?

That realization revolted real reporters who thought, researched and reasoned.

But, because they were *actual* journalists, it also put steel in their spines.

January 9, 2017; Athens, Greece, Russian Embassy

The senior diplomat at the Russian embassy in Greece, was laying his head on his desk.

His assistant walked in, saying "Mr. Ambassador?"

She screamed when she saw he was dead. Another

source for Pierre was murdered.

January 18, 2017; Washington, D.C., The White House

Every White House with an outgoing president has a party before they leave, although this was the first one since the Civil War with people openly questioning: "Can the republic survive this?"

The President was ending his goodbye remarks, noting the place his nation was in. "We are only as free as our last election."

But unable to suppress the audacity of his hope, he intoned: "But we are only as hopeful as our *next* one. Be ready for the next one."

The room applauded, sharing his hope, hope that was clouded by the knowledge of how long and perilous the road before their nation was.

The President began shaking hands around the room.

"Your Congress will never impeach," Pierre said to Jules, Zack, Max, Champion and Director Commings.

"His advisors aren't immune from prosecution," Director Commings gently reminded the Frenchman.

Hand on Pierre's shoulder, Zack said, "So far, we got the RICO charges and fraud charges for Woody. Those could form the backbone of impeachment."

"We can take a sealed Grand Jury indictment to Congress and shame them into impeaching, no?" Pierre asked. "They won't have to do a thing."

"My friend, you might overestimate what it takes to shame the House of Representatives, where impeachment begins," the Director said.

"How long can America cling to the courts and a free press?" Champion asked, not seeing the President walk up behind him.

"We better hang on to both of them with all our might," the President said. "Courts are about to be the only branch of government working, albeit the Supremes are one down."

"When the Senate confirms whoever Woody tells them to, that completes the theft of your Supreme Court, too," Pierre said sadly.

"Pierre has lost about 30 sources in the last few months," Jules said, explaining their dark mood to her – for another 48 hours-ish – commander-in-chief.

"Between me and Champ, we've lost another 50 sources in the same time frame. Every spy at Moscow station now is a rookie there."

"It is in dangerous times we should also find things that make us happy," the President said cryptically, eyes boring in on Zack.

Zack took a deep breath while the President turned Jules around by the shoulders to face Zack.

Jules was confused, then she saw Zack's face. He smiled and shrugged. He got down on one knee.

"Oh, no, get up. In front of people? What are you doing?" she smiled.

She pulled him up to her, wiggled into his chest – her left hand on his chest – and purred in his ear, "Ask me good, then put it on."

Zack smiled down at her, finding a little confidence now. "Marry me, Jules. I'm in love with you," he whispered, slipping the ring on her finger while the room applauded.

Good a spy as she was, she was out of practice. She hadn't seen this coming – and didn't see her father had now joined them in the room.

* * * *

As they said goodnight, the President effusively thanked these men and women who tried so mightily to show the world what Russia was doing to their nation.

"Thanks for having me here," Sheriff Archer said.

"I'll see you all again in the morning for the wedding," the President smiled.

* * * *

In their bedroom on Capitol Hill two hours later, Jules and Zack clung to each other tightly and orgasmed.

She wiggled out from underneath him, stretched and snuggled back next to him.

Zack grabbed her left hand, pulled it up and kissed it. They both looked at the ring.

"Still can't believe you did this," she said.

"I was sorta afraid you'd say no," he said.

"I love what we've had," she said, laying her head on his chest to hear his heartbeat. "But I also like we're gonna be legally obligated to stay that way."

She turned back over to kiss him, then interrupted it laughing, "Wait, does this mean Julianna Corday will be a U.S. citizen now?"

January 19, 2017; The White House, South Portico

In the Yellow Oval Room in the White House residence, looking out over the Truman Balcony, Sheriff Archer gazed at the Washington Monument.

President Obama walked up. "Never get tired of that."

"Never imagined I'd ever be here."

"Me either," the President laughed.

"It time?"

"Expect so," the President gestured to the door.

* * * *

At the sight of Jules on her father's arm walking through the group of friends, Zack sucked in his breath.

The President heard, and leaning over to Zack, said, "Breathe." Smiling he said, "That's generally good advice for marriage."

Zack, smiling arrogantly, whispered back in true FBI fashion, "Also before shooting."

The two suppressed a laugh.

* * * *

Afterwards, the last freely elected President of the United States looked at the group of spies and agents of Task Force Red.

He didn't know that many who would hide at Langley were disguised, lest the newly elected nationalists would discover they'd been here for the wedding and identify them for Russian assassins.

The only one of the 'Five Guys' in disguise was Max, who would be back and forth across the Atlantic.

"After tomorrow, all of you will be doing the most important work on behalf of western democracies," the commander in chief said.

"Keep documenting their crimes. Keep the Russians at bay — out of our elections. Thank you for your service and sacrifice. A blessing on this new marriage, and on your journey together."

He held up his glass in a toast, joined by the others.

Zack bent his bride over for a sexy kiss.

There were already rumors of border agents who were told to look for them to hold them in the country.

While nobody was particularly worried they could be

stopped before the new administration took over, the Director himself drove the 'Five Guys' to a Coast Guard cutter docked at the Naval Academy at Annapolis.

The Coast Guard would take them to a private yacht used by French intelligence for a sojourn to a CIA safe house in the British Virgin Islands for a honeymoon – and Champ's new nearby beachfront home, and family reunion.

Eventually, they would go north again, up the east coast, around the North Atlantic, and on to London.

January 20, 2017, Washington, D.C., the U.S. Capitol
Inaugural of the 45th President of the United States

The Chief Justice of the U.S. Supreme Court stood before Dale Woody, both with their right hands up – the Chief Justice administering the oath of office; the incoming president repeating the oath.

"And will, to the best of my ability, preserve, protect and defend the Constitution of the United States," lied the new president, who was elected by Russian spies.

He then added the line every other president had added to the constitutional oath, "So help me God."

With its familiar language, and quadrennial pomp and circumstance in the shadow of the Capitol, the audacious abnormality of this moment was almost normalizing.

Almost.

THE END

Postscript (In Real Life):

January 26, 2017: Acting Attorney General informs White House counsel that National Security Advisor made false statements about his December talks with the Russian ambassador.

✛ Alexander Kadakin, the Russian ambassador to India, died suddenly; poison is suspected.

January 27, 2017: In a private meeting, POTUS [President of the United States] asks FBI Director for "loyalty." FBI Director details meeting in writing.

January 30, 2017: POTUS fires Acting Attorney General for pointing out National Security Advisor was compromised by Russia.

February 13, 2017: POTUS fires National Security Advisor for lying about being a spy (not for being compromised).

February 14, 2017: POTUS asks FBI Director to end National Security Advisor investigation. FBI Director details meeting in writing.

✛ The Russian ambassador to the U.N. died of an apparent heart attack in his office. He was in good health.

March 2, 2017: U.S. counterintelligence learns Russia sent tailored malware to more than 10,000 DOD Twitter users — malware that took them to a Russian-controlled server for hackers to control a user's phone, computer and Twitter account.

March 7, 2017: WikiLeaks releases CIA info on hacking tools for smartphones, computers and internet-connected devices.

March 7, 2017: Nikolai Gorokhov, a Russian lawyer and anti-corruption crusader, was thrown from the fourth floor of his Moscow apartment. He survived.

March 10, 2017; Preet Bharara, Manhattan U.S. attorney, investigating Russian's Prevezon Holdings funneling Russian money into "various New York properties," is fired by POTUS.

March 30, 2017: POTUS calls FBI Director, asks him to end Russia investigation, or at least confirm he's not part of it. FBI Director details call in writing.

April 11, 2017: POTUS calls FBI Director, asks him why he hasn't confirmed POTUS is not under investigation. FBI Director details call in writing.

April 13, 2017: The Justice Department confirmed 90 instances of "concerns about voting machine malfunctions in Florida, Michigan, North Carolina, Pennsylvania, and Wisconsin" and "at least 527 responsive documents remaining in the system that relate to other types of voting issues."

Weeks leading to French election, Russian hackers are met with a vigorous anti-hacking campaign, minimizing Russia's success.

May 5, 2017, Russia releases massive document dump to undermine French candidate Emmanuel Macron.

May 7, 2017, France elects Emmanuel Macron, overcoming Russian hacking efforts.

May 9, 2017: POTUS fires FBI Director.

May 10, 2017: POTUS meets the Russian Foreign Minister and Russian Ambassador privately, saying, "I fired the head of the FBI ... because of Russia."

+ POTUS gives them highly classified intelligence about the Syrian war, busting an extraordinary Israeli spy inside ISIS.

May 11, 2017: POTUS tells NBC that he fired FBI Director over the Russia investigation.

+ Money-laundering case against Russian's Prevezon Holdings, set to go to trial in New York before Preet Bharara was fired, was suddenly settled. Russian lawyer said it was "settled on Russian terms."

May 17, 2017: Putin offers to provide the U.S. Congress with transcripts of the May 10 Oval Office conversations of POTUS, Russia's ambassador, and Russia's foreign minister.

+ Former FBI Director is named as special counsel to oversee the FBI's investigation into Russian interference with the election.

May 25, 2017: At NATO, POTUS refused to reaffirm America's pledge to mutual defense of the western alliance.

June 14, 2017: The *Washington Post* reports that special counsel is investigating POTUS for possible obstruction of justice.

July 6, 2017: Overseas, POTUS still refused to accept the unanimous conclusion of the U.S. intelligence/law enforcement community that Russia alone undermined the 2016 election.

July 7, 2017: In his first face-to-face with the new boss, POTUS forgave Putin's election engineering with a mutual promise to work together on cyber hacking – until U.S. ridicule reversed further conversations about that.

+ POTUS agreed to a "peace accord" in Syria with Putin, in Syrian area with Syrian opposition groups – not terrorists. That usually leads to wholesale slaughter of such groups by dictators.

July 13, 2017: The Kremlin recalled the Russian U.S. Ambassador back to Moscow, as investigations into Russian election interference plowed forward in 2017.

Mid July, 2017: Special counsel empaneled a grand jury, digging deeply into the financial underpinning of POTUS' private properties, including the list of shell companies and buyers of his branded real estate properties, as well as scrutinizing the roster of his tenants in New York reaching back more than a half-dozen years. The grand jury began issuing subpoenas immediately.

Then the book went to print.

ABOUT THE AUTHOR

Cathy Travis worked on Capitol Hill for 25 years as a communications director, senior advisor and political consultant for various Members of Congress until 2008.

A native of Jonesboro, Arkansas, Travis graduated from Arkansas State University and resides in Washington, D.C.

Her first book, the award-winning *Constitution Translated for Kids*, was hailed by partisans in all major political parties as an even-handed, non-ideological rendition of the founding U.S. document.

A prolific writer, Travis has written novels, children's books, nonfiction, and a screenplay based on one of her novels. Her next effort will be a screenplay based on this novel.

www.Travisbooks.com